The Three Investigators needed an afternoon off!

The young detectives wanted to take their minds off the troubles at the Crooked-Y Ranch—the mysterious accidents, the strange moaning cave, and the fears that the legendary outlaw El Diablo might have returned. So the boys set off on a leisurely stroll into town.

Suddenly they heard thundering hoofbeats behind them. They whirled to see a sinister horseman galloping down the highway. The glowering rider was dressed entirely in black—and he was aiming an ancient pistol right at the boys!

They couldn't believe their eyes. It was the terrible El Diablo—in person!

The
Mystery
of the
MOANING
CAVE

The Three Investigators
in The
Mystery
of the
MOANING
CAVE

By William Arden

Random House 🏠 New York

Originally published by Random House in 1968.
First Random House paperback edition, 1978.
Revised edition, 1985.

Library of Congress Cataloging in Publication Data:
Arden, William.
  The Three Investigators in The mystery of the moaning cave.
  (The Three Investigators mystery series ; 10)
  Rev. ed. of: Alfred Hitchcock and The Three Investigators
in The mystery of the moaning cave. 1978, c1968.
  SUMMARY: While vacationing on a California ranch,
three boys decide to investigate strange wails that come
from a mysterious cave where a famous outlaw disappeared.
  [1. Mystery and detective stories] I. Arden, William, 1924– . Alfred
Hitchcock and The Three Investigators in The mystery of the moaning
cave. II. Title. III. Title: Mystery of the moaning cave. IV. Series.
PZ7.A6794Tg   1985   [Fic]   83-26985
ISBN: 0-394-86410-7 (pbk.)

Manufactured in the United States of America
1 2 3 4 5 6 7 8 9 0

Contents

A Message from Hector Sebastian

It's my pleasure to welcome you to the latest adventure of the boys who call themselves The Three Investigators. In case you haven't met them before, let me introduce Jupiter Jones, Pete Crenshaw, and Bob Andrews. All three live in Rocky Beach, California, a small town on the Pacific Coast, near Hollywood.

A while back they formed The Three Investigators detective firm, to solve any mysteries that came their way. Which is what they've been doing ever since. The head of the company is Jupiter Jones, who has a reputation for being a genius at deduction, keeping a cool head in a crisis, and stubbornly refusing to leave any riddle alone until it's solved. The Second Investigator is Pete Crenshaw, whose athletic skill often comes in handy when the Investigators find themselves in a tight corner. Bob Andrews is the third member of the team. He's the most studious one of the group, and is in charge of records and research. The boys have set up Headquarters in an old trailer hidden from sight in The Jones Salvage Yard, a super-junkyard run by Jupiter's aunt and uncle.

While I'm at it, I'll add that I'm a writer of mysteries who has had a fair amount of success. I first encountered The Three Investigators over a case involving a missing parrot. Ever since then I've introduced their cases for them, which is exactly what I'm doing now. From time to time I pass on to them any new cases I hear about.

"We Investigate Anything" is the boys' motto. This time they prove it by traveling to a ranch in the California mountains to look into a cave that moans, a legendary outlaw who refuses to stay dead, and some rather weird events that happen in a deserted valley. What they find will make you start biting your fingernails—even if you've never done it before! So keep alert and expect the unexpected.

—HECTOR SEBASTIAN

The Mystery of the MOANING CAVE

1.

The Valley Moans

"*Aaaaaahhhhh—ooooooooooooo—ooooo—oo!*"

The eerie moan rolled out across the valley in the twilight.

"That's it," Pete Crenshaw whispered. "It's started again."

Pete, Jupiter Jones and Bob Andrews were crouched on a high ridge in a remote corner of the Crooked-Y Ranch, just a few hundred feet from the Pacific Ocean.

The moan came again, long, drawn-out and chilling. "*Aaaaaaaaaaahhhh—oooooooooooo—oooo!*"

A shiver ran up Pete's spine. "I don't blame the ranch hands for not wanting to come here any more," he said to his companions.

3

"Maybe it comes from the lighthouse we saw on the way," Bob suggested in a low tone. "Maybe it's some kind of echo from the foghorn."

Jupiter shook his head. "No, Bob, I don't think it's the lighthouse. The sound is not that of a foghorn signal. Besides, there isn't any fog this evening."

"Then what——" Bob began, but Jupiter was no longer crouched beside him. The stocky First Investigator was trotting off to the right along the ridge. Pete and Bob leaped up and followed. The sun was almost gone now in the crevasse between the coast mountains, and a hazy purple light hung over the valley.

Jupiter stopped after some fifty yards. The moan came again. He listened carefully, his hand cupped behind his ear.

Pete stared, puzzled. "What are we doing, Jupe?"

Jupiter didn't answer. Instead he turned and walked almost a hundred yards in the opposite direction.

"Are we just going to walk all over this ridge, Jupe?" Bob asked, as puzzled as Pete by Jupiter's strange actions.

Before Jupiter could reply, another eerie moan floated through the valley. "*Aaaaahhhhhhh—oooooooooo—oooo!*"

Jupiter turned to them. "No, Bob, we've completed the experiment."

"What experiment?" Pete blurted out. "We haven't been doing anything but walk!"

"We have listened to the moan from three different points on this ridge," Jupiter explained. "In my mind I drew imaginary lines from where I listened to where the moans appeared to originate. Where the three lines crossed is the exact source of the sound."

Bob suddenly understood. "Sure, Pete," he said. "It's called triangulation. Engineers use it all the time."

"Precisely," Jupiter said. "Of course, the way I did it was very rough, but it will serve our purpose."

"What purpose, Jupe?" asked Pete. "I mean, what did we find out?"

"We have found that the exact source of the sound is that cave in the mountain—El Diablo's Cave," Jupiter announced.

"Hey, Jupe," Pete exclaimed, "we knew that already. Mr. and Mrs. Dalton told us."

Jupiter shook his head. "Good investigators do not accept what other people report without checking it themselves. Witnesses are often unreliable, as Mr. Sebastian has told us many times."

Jupiter referred to the famous mystery writer, Hector Sebastian, who had been a good friend of The Three Investigators ever since the boys had discovered the whereabouts of a missing parrot that belonged to a friend of his.

"I guess you're right," Pete said. "Mr. Sebastian showed us how little witnesses really see."

"Or hear," Jupiter added. "But now I have no doubt that the moaning does come from El Diablo's Cave. All we have to do is find out what is moaning, and——"

The stocky boy did not finish his sentence, for the moan rolled out once more—weird and chilling in the deep twilight of the shadowy valley. "*Aaaaaahhhhhh—ooooooooooooo—oooooo—oo!*"

Even Jupiter shivered this time, as long shadows began to creep across the valley.

Pete swallowed hard. "Jupe, Mr. Dalton and the sheriff have searched the cave three times already. They didn't find anything."

"Maybe it's some kind of animal," Bob volunteered.

"It doesn't sound like any animal I ever heard," replied Jupiter, "and, anyway, the sheriff and Mr. Dalton would have found traces of any normal animal. They're expert hunters and trackers."

"Any *normal* animal?" Pete repeated uneasily.

"Maybe it's some animal no one knows is here," Jupiter said. "Or maybe," and the First Investigator's eyes sparkled, "it's El Diablo himself!"

"Oh, no you don't!" Pete cried. "We don't believe in ghosts—do we?"

Jupiter grinned. "Who said anything about ghosts?"

"But El Diablo's been dead almost a hundred

years," Bob objected. "If you don't mean a ghost, Jupe, what do you mean?"

Jupiter did not get a chance to answer, for at that moment the sky beyond the valley was suddenly lit up by bright red flashes. The boys' eyes widened as explosions seemed to shake the whole valley.

"What is it, Jupe?" asked Bob.

Jupiter shook his head. "I don't know."

The flashes stopped and the echo of the explosions faded away. The three boys looked at each other. Then Bob snapped his fingers.

"I know, it's the Navy! Remember when we were coming up on the truck, Jupe, we saw all those Navy ships on practice maneuvers? I'll bet they're having target practice out in the Channel Islands."

Pete laughed with relief. "Sure, they do that a couple of times a year. I read about it in the newspapers. They fire at some uninhabited island out there."

Jupiter nodded. "It was even in the papers yesterday. Night firing practice. Come on, I want to get back to the ranch and find out more about this valley."

Bob and Pete needed no urging, for the valley had now grown completely dark. The three boys walked to their bikes, which were parked on the dirt road behind them.

Suddenly, from across the valley, they heard a loud rumbling sound, followed by a long wail.

2.
The Old One

The wail died away across Moaning Valley.

"That wasn't the moan from the cave!" cried Pete.

"No," Jupiter agreed. "That was a man!"

"In trouble," added Bob. "Come on, fellows!"

The sound had come from the base of the mountain that stood between the valley and the ocean—Devil Mountain, so-called because of its jagged twin peaks shaped like horns.

The boys raced across the valley to the foot of Devil Mountain, where a pile of newly fallen rocks lay strewn across the slope. Dust still filled the air.

"Help!" a voice called feebly.

Pete knelt down beside the gray-haired man who lay there, his leg twisted at a strange angle beneath the rocks, his face contorted with pain. "Just lie quietly," Pete told him. "We'll get you out of here right away."

Pete stood up and looked at Jupiter. "I think his leg is broken. We'd better go for help quickly."

The man on the ground was dressed in the old work clothes of a ranch hand. He gritted his teeth as he spoke.

"You boys go to The Crooked-Y ranch house. I work there. Tell Mr. Dalton to get some men out here."

The boys looked at each other in dismay. Another accident for one of Mr. Dalton's men! More trouble in Moaning Valley!

Pete had come to The Crooked-Y to spend a two-week vacation with Mr. and Mrs. Dalton, the new owners of the ranch. Jess Dalton, a famous rodeo rider who had worked with Mr. Crenshaw in several Western movies, had decided to retire and buy a ranch with his lifetime savings. The Daltons were barely getting started on rebuilding the rundown ranch when the trouble began.

Moaning Valley, which had earned its strange name from ancient Indian legends and some violent events of old Spanish days, had begun to moan again —after fifty years of silence. As if this was not enough to scare the hired ranch hands, the accidents had started.

The first accident occurred while two of the

ranch hands were riding through Moaning Valley at dusk one evening. They suddenly heard a strange moaning noise, and their horses bolted, throwing both men. One of the men broke his arm, and both returned to the ranch talking about how there was "something spooky in that valley." Soon after, a herd of cattle stampeded for no apparent reason in the middle of the night. Then a ranch hand walking in the valley at dusk swore he had seen a giant shape emerge from El Diablo's Cave at the base of Devil Mountain. Shortly after that, two hands disappeared without any explanation and, though the sheriff insisted that he had found them in nearby Santa Carla, many of the ranch hands had refused to believe him.

Pete hadn't been at the ranch very long before he realized that the Daltons were extremely worried. Searches of the cave had revealed no explanation, and the sheriff could not pursue ghosts or legends. Both he and Mr. Dalton were sure there was some simple explanation, but so far no one had been able to find it. So Pete had hurriedly sent for Bob and Jupiter, explaining that there was a possible mystery for the Three Investigators to solve. The two boys had no trouble getting permission to come to the ranch, and the Daltons were glad to have them.

The Crooked-Y was located only ten miles from the modern resort city of Santa Carla, and less than a hundred miles north of Rocky Beach on the California coast. The countryside consisted of rugged mountains, deep valleys and canyons, with isolated coves along the Pacific coast. Bob's parents and Jupiter's aunt and uncle had thought it a fine idea for the boys to have a chance to see a real ranch and go riding, swimming and fishing.

But the boys were not riding or fishing or swimming; they were investigating the mystery of Moaning Valley. And that was how they had discovered the man who lay there on the ground, his leg caught beneath the pile of fallen rocks.

"It's this jinxed valley, that's what it is," the man muttered in pain. "I never should have come here. . . . That moaning, that's what did it."

"No, I don't think so," Jupiter said seriously. "I think the shock of the naval firing loosened some stones and the slide resulted. The side of Devil Mountain is very dry and quite steep."

"It was that moaning!" the injured man insisted.

"We'd really better get some help, fellows," Pete said. "We can't get those rocks off him alone."

Just then a horse whinnied close by. The boys turned to see three men riding over the top of the valley toward them. One of the men led a riderless horse. The lead rider was Mr. Dalton himself.

"What are you boys doing here?" Mr. Dalton demanded as he dismounted. He was a tall, wiry man in a bright red shirt, faded blue jeans, and tooled, high-heeled western boots. His tanned, leathery face was lined with worry.

The boys explained how they had found the injured man.

"How do you feel, Cardigo?" Mr. Dalton asked, as he knelt down beside the ranch hand.

"I've got a broken leg," mumbled the man, "and it's this jinxed valley that did it. I'm getting out."

"I think the firing of the guns loosened some rocks and started the slide," Jupiter explained.

"Of course," Mr. Dalton agreed. "That was it. Hold still now, Cardigo, and we'll have you loose in a jiffy."

Moments later they had removed the rocks from the injured man, and the two ranch hands had gone for the truck. They backed up to the rock slide and carefully lifted Cardigo into the back. The truck drove off for the hospital in Santa Carla, and the three boys returned to their bikes.

It was completely dark by the time Bob, Pete and Jupiter rode up to the ranch house and parked their bikes. Altogether there were five ranch buildings: a bunkhouse for the hands, a large barn, a smaller barn, a cookhouse, and the main house. The main house was an old, two-story, wood-beam and adobe structure surrounded by a deep, cool porch. The whole house was covered with the bright red flowers of trumpet vine, and the deep red blooms of bougainvillaea. Fenced corrals surrounded the entire group of buildings.

Men were gathered in small groups around the cookhouse, obviously talking about the accident. Their voices were low, but their faces showed fear and anger.

The boys were about to go into the main house

when a voice came out of the night—a deep, harsh voice.

"What have you boys been up to?"

On the porch something moved and the boys made out the small, wiry form and sharp, weather-lined face of Luke Hardin, the ranch foreman.

"Big place, this ranch," Hardin said. "Get lost mighty easy."

"We're used to open country and mountains, Mr. Hardin," Jupiter replied. "You don't have to worry about us."

The foreman took a step toward them. "I heard what you've been up to. Moanin' Valley, that's what. That place ain't fit for youngsters, hear? You stay away from there!"

Before the boys could protest, the door of the ranch house opened and a small, peppery woman with gray hair and a deeply tanned face bustled out.

"Nonsense, Luke!" Mrs. Dalton snapped. "The boys aren't children. They seem to have a heap more sense than you do."

"Moanin' Valley ain't a good place," Hardin said stubbornly.

"A grown man like you," Mrs. Dalton exclaimed. "Afraid of a cave!"

"I ain't afraid," Hardin said slowly. "But I ain't afraid to face facts, neither. I lived around here all my life. Even when I was a boy I heard about Moanin' Valley. I never believed the stories then, but now I ain't so sure."

"Fiddlesticks! It's just old superstition and you

know it!" Mrs. Dalton said. Though she spoke bravely, Mrs. Dalton couldn't quite hide the fact that she, too, was worried.

"What do *you* think causes the moaning, Mr. Hardin?" Jupiter asked the foreman.

The foreman squinted gravely at Jupiter. "Don't know, boy. No one else does, either. We've looked, but no one's found anything. Nothin' we could *see*, that is."

The foreman's eyes seemed to glow in the dark. "Indians always did say that no one could see The Old One!"

3.
El Diablo's Escape

"Luke!" Mrs. Dalton cried.

But the foreman stood his ground. "I ain't saying I believe the stories. But a man's got to look straight at things. That cave's started moanin' again, but so far nobody's found nothin' to explain it. If it ain't The Old One, what do *you* reckon it is?"

With that, Luke Hardin walked down off the porch toward the bunkhouse. Mrs. Dalton stared after him with a worried expression.

"I'm afraid this is affecting all of us," Mrs. Dalton said. "Luke's as brave a man as I ever saw. I never heard him talk that way before."

"I wonder why he decided to talk to us about The Old One?" Jupiter asked thoughtfully.

Mrs. Dalton suddenly smiled. "I expect Luke's just tired. We've all been worried and working too hard. Now, what do you boys say to some milk and cookies?"

es, ma'am!" Pete answered quickly for all of

Soon the boys were eating cookies in the comfortable living room of the old ranch house. Colorful Indian rugs covered the floor under the rustic hand-hewn furniture, and a large stone fireplace almost filled one wall. The mounted heads of deer, bear, and mountain lions hung on the walls.

"Just what *is* The Old One, Mrs. Dalton?" Jupiter asked, helping himself to another cookie.

"An old Indian legend, Jupiter, nothing more. When the Spaniards first came here a very long time ago the local Indians said that a black and shiny monster called The Old One lived in a pool deep inside the cave in Devil Mountain."

Pete blinked. "But if no one could see The Old One, how did they know it was black and shiny?"

Mrs. Dalton laughed. "There, you see? Of course it doesn't make sense. I suppose they believed that someone had once seen the thing and told others about it, and that's how the story was handed down."

"What did the Spaniards think?" Bob asked.

"Well, that was a long time ago," Mrs. Dalton said, "and they were pretty superstitious, too. They said they didn't believe it but they never went near the valley if they could help it. Only the very bravest, like El Diablo himself, went into the cave."

"Can you tell us about El Diablo?" Jupiter asked.

At that moment Mr. Dalton entered the room, accompanied by a small, thin man who wore heavy glasses. The boys had met the man earlier. He was a house guest of the Daltons, Professor Walsh.

"Ah, boys, I hear that you have been out at our mysterious Moaning Valley," said the professor.

"Foolishness!" Mr. Dalton snapped. "Nothing has happened there that doesn't happen on any ranch. Simple accidents, nothing more."

"Of course you're right," Professor Walsh said, "but I'm afraid your men don't believe that. Uneducated people would rather believe in supernatural forces than in their own carelessness."

"If only we could find the cause and show them," Mr. Dalton said. "After this accident tonight I'll lose more men. But even Jupiter here could see that the slide was caused by that naval gunfire off the coast."

"Excuse me, sir," Jupiter interrupted, "but we would like to help if we could. We've had some experience in this sort of thing, as Mr. Crenshaw may have told you."

"Experience?" Mr. Dalton repeated, staring at the boys.

Jupiter produced two cards from his pocket and handed them to Mr. Dalton. The tall rancher studied them. The first, a large business card said:

THE THREE INVESTIGATORS
"We Investigate Anything"
?   ?   ?

First Investigator . . . . . . Jupiter Jones
Second Investigator . . . Peter Crenshaw
Records and Research . . . Bob Andrews

Mr. Dalton frowned. "Investigators, eh? Well, I don't know, boys. The sheriff might not like boys interfering."

Professor Walsh looked at the card. "Why the question marks, boys? Do you doubt your ability as detectives?"

The professor smiled at his own joke, but Bob and Pete only grinned and waited for Jupe to explain. Adults always asked about the question marks, which was exactly what Jupiter wanted.

"No sir," Jupiter said. "The question marks are our symbol. They stand for questions unanswered, mysteries unsolved, enigmas of all sorts that we attempt to unravel. So far we have never failed to explain any riddle we've found."

Jupiter said the last proudly. But Mr. Dalton was looking at the second card, a small green one. Each of the boys had one, and they all read the same:

This certifies that the bearer is a Volunteer Junior Assistant Deputy cooperating with the Police Force of Rocky Beach. Any assistance given him will be appreciated.

Samuel Reynolds
Chief of Police

Professor Walsh peered at the card through his thick glasses. "Well, well. Very impressive, boys. You do indeed have fine credentials."

"You boys certainly showed more sense tonight

than half the adults around here," Mr. Dalton said at last. "Maybe three boys with a fresh viewpoint are just what we need to solve this nonsense. I'm sure there's a simple explanation, and if you promise to be very careful around that cave, I say go ahead and investigate."

"We'll be careful!" the boys cried in unison.

Mrs. Dalton smiled. "I'm sure there's some very simple explanation we've all missed."

Mr. Dalton snorted. "I say it's the wind blowing through those old tunnels and nothing more."

Jupiter finished the last cookie. "You and the sheriff have searched the cave, sir?"

"From one end to the other. Many of the passages are blocked by debris from old earthquakes, but we searched every one we could find."

"Did you find anything that looked as if it had changed recently?" Jupiter questioned.

"Changed?" Mr. Dalton frowned. "Nothing we could see. What are you getting at, son?"

"Well, sir," Jupiter explained, "I understand that the moaning only began a month ago. Before that it hadn't been heard for at least fifty years. If the wind is causing the sound, then it seems only logical that something must have changed inside the cave to make the moaning sound start again. I mean, I doubt if the *wind* has changed."

"Hah!" Professor Walsh said. "There's clear logic, Dalton. Perhaps these boys *can* solve your mystery."

Jupiter ignored the interruption. "I also understand," he went on, "that the moaning occurs only at night, which would not be the case if the wind alone were responsible. Have you noticed if it happens every windy night, by any chance?"

"No, I don't think it does, Jupiter." Mr. Dalton was beginning to look really interested. "I see what you mean. If it were just the wind, then we should hear moaning *every* windy night. . . . Of course, it could be a combination of wind and some special atmospheric condition."

Professor Walsh smiled. "Or it could be El Diablo, come back to ride again!"

Pete gulped. "Don't say that, Professor. Jupe already said the same thing!"

Professor Walsh looked over at Jupiter. "He did, did he? You're not going to tell me that *you* believe in ghosts, are you, young man?"

"No one knows about ghosts for sure, sir," Bob put in seriously. "However, we've never actually found a real ghost."

"I see," the professor said. "Well, the Spanish people have always insisted that El Diablo will come back when he is needed. I've done a great deal of research, and I can't really say that he couldn't come back."

"Research?" Bob asked.

"Professor Walsh is a professor of history," Mrs. Dalton explained. "He's here in Santa Carla for a year to do special research on California history. Mr. Dalton thought he might be able to help us explain Moaning Valley to our ranch hands."

"With no luck so far," the professor admitted. "But perhaps you boys would be interested in the full story of El Diablo? I'm thinking of writing a book on his colorful career."

"That would be great!" Bob exclaimed.

"Yes, I would like to hear more about him," Jupiter agreed.

Professor Walsh leaned back in his chair and began to tell the story of El Diablo and his famous last adventure.

In the early days of California the land that now made up The Crooked-Y Ranch had been part of the Delgado Rancho. The estate of the Delgado family had been one of the largest land-grants given to the Spanish settlers by the King of Spain. The Spaniards did not come to California in large numbers, as the English did in the eastern part of America. So the Delgado Rancho remained a vast private domain for many generations.

Then settlers began to come to California from the East, and slowly the land of the Delgados was given away, lost, or stolen. After the Mexican War, California became part of the United States, and more and more Americans arrived to settle the land, especially after the great Gold Rush of 1849. By 1880 almost all the great domain of the Delgados was gone, except a small area about the size of The Crooked-Y that included Moaning Valley.

The last of the Delgados, Gaspar Ortèga Jesus de Delgado y Cabrillo, was a brave and fiery young man who grew up hating the American settlers. He thought of them as thieves who had stolen his family's land. Young Gaspar had little money and no power, but he longed to avenge his family and regain his land. He decided to become the champion of all the old Spanish-Mexican families who had been in California so long. Hiding out in the hills, he became an outlaw. To the Spanish people he was a new Robin Hood. To the Americans he was nothing more than a bandit.

The Americans named Gaspar Delgado *El Diablo*—The Devil—after the mountain where he had his cave headquarters. But for two years they could not catch him. He stole tax money, scared away tax collectors, raided American government offices and stole their funds, and generally helped the Spanish-speaking Californians and terrorized the Americans.

But in 1888 El Diablo was finally captured by the sheriff of Santa Carla County. In a famous trial, which the Spanish-speaking people said was a fake, he was sentenced to hang. Then, two days before he was to be executed, some friends helped him in a daring daylight escape. El Diablo climbed over the roof of the courthouse, jumped several feet to another roof, and finally leaped to the back of his waiting black horse.

Wounded in his escape, and closely pursued by the sheriff and his posse, El Diablo rode to his hide-out in the cave in Moaning Valley. The sheriff and his men blocked all known exits, but they did not go inside. They thought that El Diablo would have to come out when he became hungry, or when his wound became too painful to endure.

Though they stood watch for several days, there was no sign of El Diablo. But all the time they waited, they heard a strange moaning coming from somewhere inside the cave. Naturally they assumed that the moans came from the wounded bandit. Finally the sheriff ordered his men inside. They searched every passage and cavern for four days, but found nothing. They searched the whole countryside, too. But they never uncovered a trace of El Diablo—not him, or his body, or his clothes, or his pistol, or his horse, or his money. Nothing.

El Diablo was never seen again. Some said that his faithful sweetheart, Dolores de Castillo, had gone into the cave through a secret entrance and helped him escape, and that they had fled far away to a new life in South America. Others said that friends spirited him out and then hid him in *rancho* after *rancho* for many years.

But most people said that El Diablo never left the cave, that he simply remained hidden where the Americans could not find him, and that he was still there! For many years, every time there was an unsolved robbery or act of violence, it was said to have been El Diablo, still riding through the night on his great black horse. The moaning continued somewhere inside the cave, which became known as El Diablo's Cave.

"Then," Professor Walsh concluded, "the moaning suddenly stopped. The Spanish-speaking people said that El Diablo had grown weary and given up his raids—but that he was still in the cave waiting for a time when he would be really needed!"

"Gosh," Pete exclaimed. "You mean some people think he's still there in the cave?"

"How could he be?" Bob asked.

"Well, boys," the professor said, "I've done a great deal of research on El Diablo. For example, all his old pictures show him wearing his pistol on the right hip, but I am certain he was left-handed!"

Jupiter nodded thoughtfully. "The stories about such a legendary figure are often false."

"Exactly," Professor Walsh said. "Now the official story has always been that he died of his wound that night in the cave. But I have studied the record closely, and I am convinced that his wound could not have been fatal. Since he was only eighteen years old in 1888, it is entirely possible that El Diablo is still alive!"

4.
The Investigation Begins

"Don't be ridiculous, Walsh!" Mr. Dalton exploded. "Why, that would make him almost a hundred years old. A man that old isn't likely to be running around the countryside!"

"I think you'd be surprised how spry a man of a hundred can be," Professor Walsh said quietly. "There are reports of men in the Caucasus Mountains of southern Russia who still ride and fight when they are a hundred or more. Anyway, our phantom isn't doing much more than moan from a cave."

"That's true, sir," Jupiter said.

"Also," Professor Walsh pointed out, "it is entirely possible that El Diablo might have descendants. Perhaps a son or even a grandson is carrying on his career."

Mr. Dalton began to look a little less skeptical. "That sounds more likely. The people who had the ranch before us never used Moaning Valley, but we are planning to build a range corral out there. Perhaps some descendant doesn't want El Diablo's legend interfered with."

"Jess, that could be the answer!" Mrs. Dalton cried. "Don't you remember? Some of our older Mexican ranch hands were against our plan to use Moaning Valley even before the moaning began."

"And they were among the first to leave us," Mr. Dalton exclaimed. "Tomorrow I'm going to talk to the sheriff and see if he knows of any descendants of El Diablo."

"Perhaps you'd all like to see a picture of El Diablo," Professor Walsh said. He took a small picture from his pocket and passed it around. It showed a slim young man with burning, dark eyes and a proud face. The picture, which was obviously a photograph of a painting, seemed to prove that El Diablo had been little more than a boy. He wore a wide-brimmed, high-crowned black *vaquero* sombrero, a short black jacket, a black shirt with a high neck, and tight black trousers that flared at the bottom above shiny black pointed boots.

"Did he always wear black?" Bob asked.

"Always," Walsh replied. "He said that he was in mourning for his people and his country."

"He was a bandit and nothing more, and tomorrow I'll talk to the sheriff to see if any fools are trying to continue his legend," Mr. Dalton said firmly. Then the lean rancher smiled. "And interesting as I admit El Diablo is, a ranch doesn't run itself. I have work to do tonight, and you boys must be tired from your trip. I expect I'll be working you hard tomorrow. Pete's Dad said you wanted to learn all about how a ranch operates, and the only way to learn is to do the work."

"We're really not at all tired, Mr. Dalton," Jupiter said briskly. "Are we, fellows?"

"Not at all," Bob agreed.

"Gosh, no," Pete echoed.

"It's still early, and a clear night," Jupe went on, "and we'd like to look around the ranch as much as we can. The beach is especially interesting at night. There's some remarkable flora and fauna up here along the sea that only appears at night."

Mr. and Mrs. Dalton looked impressed. Jupiter's correct use of so many big words always made adults think that he must be older than he actually was. Bob and Pete, however, were aware that Jupe had more on his mind than a walk along the beach. They tried to look as wide awake as possible.

"Well . . . " Mrs. Dalton began dubiously.

"Why not, boys?" Mr. Dalton decided. "It's early, and I expect the first night on a ranch is too exciting to be wasted in sleep." He turned to his wife. "Do them good, Martha. Better to look around the beach tonight, because I'll be keeping them pretty busy starting tomorrow."

"All right then." Mrs. Dalton smiled. "Off with you, but no later than ten o'clock. We get up early here."

The three boys did not wait for further talk. They carried their cookie plates and milk glasses to the kitchen and went out the back door.

As soon as they were out of the house, Jupiter started to give instructions. "Pete, you go to the barn and get that long coil of rope I saw hanging there. Bob, you go up to our room and get our chalk and our flashlights. I'll get our bikes ready."

"Are we going to the cave, Jupe?" Bob asked.

"Right. That is the only place to solve the mystery of Moaning Valley."

"The cave?" Pete gulped. "Now? Couldn't we see more in the daytime?"

"The moaning only happens at night," Jupiter pointed out, "and when you're inside a cave daytime doesn't make any difference. Besides, the cave doesn't moan every night. We know that it's been moaning tonight, and if we don't go now we might have to wait for days."

By this time the other two were convinced. They moved swiftly into operation, and shortly afterward the three boys met at the ranch gate.

Pete tied the long coil of rope to his luggage carrier, and they bicycled away along the narrow dirt road. The night was warm and the moon was up now, shining down on the silvery road that lay ahead.

Although the Crooked-Y Ranch stretched for miles along the shore of the Pacific Ocean, the sea itself was hidden by the coastal mountains. In the moonlight the rocky mountains were tall and silent, and the green live-oak trees looked like pale white ghosts. As they rode, the boys could hear the herds of cattle moving restlessly in the fields, the horses snorting and whinnying close to the road.

Then suddenly, without warning, the eerie moan floated out across the valley.

"*Aaaaaaaaaaaahhhhhhh—ooooooooooooooooo—ooooooooo—oo!*"

Even though they had expected it, Pete and Bob both jumped nervously.

"Good," whispered Jupiter. "The moaning hasn't stopped."

They quietly parked their bikes and from the high ridge looked across the moonlit valley at the dark opening of El Diablo's Cave.

"Gosh, Jupe," Bob said. "I keep thinking I see things moving."

"And I hear noises," Pete added.

"Yes," Jupiter said firmly. "But that is your imagination. In eerie surroundings like these, the simplest sound seems frightening. Now are we all ready? Bob, check the flashlights again."

Bob tested the flashlights and Pete looped the rope over his shoulder. Each boy took his piece of chalk in his hand.

"Caves can be dangerous unless you take the

proper precautions," Jupiter explained. "The main dangers are falling into chasms and becoming lost. We have the rope in case any of us fall, and by marking our trail with chalk no one will become lost. We will stay together at all times."

"Shall we mark our trail with question marks?"

"Right," Jupiter said. "And we will also use arrows to indicate the direction we have taken." The question marks in chalk were one of his most inspired inventions. The boys used them to leave a trail. The marks instantly made it clear that one of the investigators had been in a place. Since Jupiter's chalk was white, Pete's blue, and Bob's green, it was even possible to tell exactly which one had made the marks.

"Well," Pete said. "Are we ready?"

"I believe we are," Jupiter said, satisfied at last.

The boys took a deep breath, and then began to walk down the slope of the ridge into the valley.

Once more the moan wailed out in the night. "*Aaaaaahhhhhhhh—oooooooooooo—oooooo—oo!*"

A swift current of cold air came to meet them as they neared the dark opening of the cave. Jupiter, in the lead, had already switched on his flashlight when suddenly he heard a rumbling sound.

"What's that?" Bob cried.

The sound grew louder. Because of the strange echoing effect in the bowl-shaped valley, it seemed to come from all around them.

"Look up there!" Pete shouted, pointing.

A giant boulder was tumbling down the steep

face of Devil Mountain in a shower of smaller stones.

"Jump!" Pete cried.

Bob hurled himself sideways out of the path of the hurtling boulder.

But Jupiter stood frozen, staring at the great rock as it fell straight down toward him.

5.
El Diablo's Cave

Pete threw himself at Jupiter, knocking the First Investigator away from the mouth of the cave. The boulder struck the ground with shattering force directly where Jupiter had been standing.

Bob scrambled to his feet. "Are you all right?" he asked anxiously.

Pete stood up. "I think so. Are you, Jupe?"

Jupiter got up more slowly and brushed at his clothes. His eyes had that faraway look that they always got when he was thinking.

"I was unable to move. A most interesting mental reaction," he mused. "It's similar to the way a small animal becomes paralyzed when a snake looks at it. The animal literally can't move, and is easily caught when it could have escaped."

Bob and Pete both stared at their friend as he coolly analyzed such a narrow escape from injury. Jupiter gazed up at the side of Devil Mountain in the moonlight.

"There seem to be many loose boulders up there," Jupe observed, "and the mountainside is very dry. I imagine it's quite common for rocks to fall here. The naval gunnery probably loosened them in many places."

The three boys approached the big rock. It was buried deep in the ground only a few yards from the entrance to El Diablo's cave.

"Look, there are marks on it!" Bob was pointing at the boulder. "Gosh, Jupe, do you think someone pushed it down on us?"

"There *are* some marks," Jupiter said after he had examined the rock more carefully. "Of course that is not so surprising."

"It hit against a lot of other rocks on its way down," Pete pointed out.

"We didn't see anyone up there," Bob said.

Jupiter nodded. "Still, someone up there might not want to be seen."

"Gee, maybe we better go back," Pete said.

"No, but we'll be even more careful," Jupiter said. "At least rocks can't fall down a mountain at us when we're inside the cave."

With Jupiter in the lead, the boys entered the cave. They turned on their flashlights, and Bob marked the first question mark and arrow at the entrance.

Even with their flashlights on, they could see nothing but a long, dark passage that went straight into Devil Mountain. Its walls were smooth, and the ceiling was just high enough to permit Pete—the tallest investigator—to stand up. For a distance of about forty feet the passageway continued to be a straight tunnel with smooth stone walls. Then it suddenly opened into a large cavern.

The boys shone their flashlights around them. They were in a huge room with a towering ceiling. The far end of the cavern was so distant they could only just see it.

"It's like a big-city railroad station!" Bob exclaimed. "I never saw a cave so big." His voice sounded hollow and faraway.

"Hello!" Pete called.

"Hello . . . hello . . . hello-ooooooo," his voice echoed.

The boys laughed. The echoes seemed to bounce through the cavern. *"Hello . . . hello-ooooo!"* shouted Bob.

While Pete and Bob were shouting, Jupiter was inspecting the huge cavern more closely with the help of his flashlight.

"Look!" he suddenly called to them.

To their left, in the wall, was a small black hole —the opening of a passage that seemed to lead out of the cavern. The boys aimed their flashlights at the walls on both sides of the cavern. They saw many more openings—at least ten passages that led from the big cavern deeper into the mountain.

"Wow," Pete said, "which way do we go?"

All the passages looked about the same—barely high enough for Pete to stand up in, and about four feet wide.

Jupiter frowned. "It is obvious that El Diablo's Cave must be a large complex of passages and chambers all through the mountain."

"Maybe that's why the posse couldn't find El Diablo," Bob said. "There were so many passages that he could stay hidden."

Jupiter nodded. "A likely explanation."

"How does a cave like this get started anyway?" Pete asked, looking around with awe.

"Water erosion mainly," Bob explained. "I've read about it in the library. A mountain like this is made up of different rocks, some softer than the others. The water seeps in and wears away the softer rock. It takes millions of years sometimes. A lot of this area was under water a long time ago."

"Bob's right," Jupiter said. "But I'm not sure that all of these passages are natural. Some of them look man-made. Maybe by El Diablo's men."

"Or miners, Jupe," Bob said. "I read how they used to look for gold around here."

Pete was shining his light at first one passage, then another. "Where do we start looking?" he asked.

"It could take us months to search all these passages," said Bob. "I'll bet each one branches out again farther on."

"Probably," Jupiter agreed, "but fortunately we have an easy way to eliminate some of them. We're looking for the moaning sound. All we have to do is listen at each entrance until we find the one where the moaning is coming from."

"Hey, that's right," Pete said with enthusiasm. "We'll just follow the moaning."

"But Jupe . . ." Bob was looking puzzled. "The moaning. I don't hear it. I mean, I haven't heard it since we came inside!"

The three boys stood perfectly still, listening intently. Bob was right—the cave was as quiet as a tomb.

"Jupe?" Pete said uneasily. "What does it mean?"

Jupiter shook his head in puzzlement. "I don't know. Maybe it's just a coincidence. Maybe it'll start again soon."

But the moaning did not start. Ten minutes passed and there was no sound inside the cave.

"I remember hearing it just before that rock fell, Jupe," said Bob. "Only I wasn't listening much after that."

"We were too excited to think about it," Jupiter said. "We can't really be sure when it stopped."

"Gosh," Pete said, "what do we do now?"

"Perhaps it will begin again," Jupiter said hopefully. "Mr. Dalton did say the cave moans irregularly. While we're waiting, I think we should start to search the side passages one by one."

Bob and Pete agreed. Anything would be better than just standing there in the spooky darkness. Bob chalked a question mark and an arrow at the entrance to the first side passage, and the boys entered the tunnel.

They moved cautiously, their flashlights probing ahead until, less than thirty feet from the entrance, the tunnel suddenly ended. It did not end in a blank wall but in a pile of fallen rock that completely blocked the passage.

"Mr. Dalton said many of the tunnels were blocked by old earthquakes," Bob recalled.

Pete looked worried. "Do you think it's still dangerous?"

"No," Jupiter said. "The ceilings are very solid. It took a heavy shock to make these rocks fall, and then only the very weakest places fell. This is a very safe cave."

They retraced their steps, and tried the next four tunnels, carefully marking each entrance. All four passages ended in piles of fallen rocks.

"We're wasting time," said Jupiter finally. "We'll split up and each search a passage. They seem quite safe."

"We'll each go through our tunnel until we can see the end," Bob agreed, "unless it turns out not to be blocked."

"That's it," Jupiter said. "If one of us finds a clear passage he can come back and wait here for the others."

Quickly, each of the boys plunged into a tunnel, hopefully shining his flashlight ahead.

Jupiter found that his passage was natural for only a short distance. Then his flashlight revealed beams and braces that held up the walls, as in a mine shaft. He moved ahead cautiously for a few more yards, studying the floor and walls of the shaft.

Abruptly he came to a wall of rock and dirt that blocked the passage. Kneeling down to inspect the barricade more closely, he discovered a small, hard black stone that puzzled him. It was quite different from any stone he had ever seen. He stuck it into his pocket to examine later.

Just then a yell echoed through the passage. "Jupe! Bob! Hurry!"

At that moment Bob was in another large cavern similar to the first they had found. The tunnel he had been exploring had led him straight into the cavern. He was standing there dismayed because this one, too, had many small passages that led out of it. He had just decided to return to the first cavern and wait for the others when he heard Pete's yell. Immediately he rushed back to the entrance of his tunnel.

Meanwhile, Jupiter was racing toward the mouth of Pete's tunnel. Suddenly something came hurtling at him out of the dark. The next thing he knew he was sprawled on the stone floor with some wild creature clawing at him.

"Help!" a voice called in fright.

The voice was almost in Jupiter's ear. It was Bob's voice.

"Bob, it's me!" cried Jupiter.

The hands that were clawing at Jupe relaxed, and the two boys shone their lights on each other.

"Gosh, I thought something had grabbed me," Bob said.

"My reaction was the same." Jupiter said. "It was a case of panic brought on by Pete's call for——"

"Pete!" Bob cried.

"Come on!" said Jupe.

The two boys raced into the passage Pete had taken. The tunnel seemed longer than the others. They had been running for some distance before they saw a light ahead. It was coming from Pete's flashlight.

"Here I am!" Pete called.

Bob and Jupiter burst out of the passage into still another large cavern. Pete stood in the center, the beam of his flashlight trained on the left wall. He was looking pale.

"There was . . . something in here!" Pete stammered. "I saw it. All black and shiny!"

Bob and Jupiter focused their flashlights on the wall. They could see nothing at all.

"I tell you I saw something," Pete insisted.

"When I came out of the tunnel I heard a noise. I shone my light and saw . . . this . . . thing! Over there near the wall. It was big. I was so surprised I dropped my light, and when I picked it up the thing was gone."

Bob looked skeptical. "Maybe you were just nervous, Pete. We shouldn't have split up."

But Jupiter walked over to the wall where Pete said he had seen the black, shiny shape. He knelt down.

"Pete wasn't just nervous, Bob," Jupiter said. "Look here."

Pete and Bob hurried to where Jupe was kneeling. There were two large, dark marks on the stone floor. Big, egg-shaped footprints that reflected the bright beam of the flashlight.

"What . . ." Bob hesitated. "What is it, Jupe?"

"Something wet," Jupiter said. "Water probably, but it might be something else."

"Ugh." Pete gulped.

Jupiter shone his light all across the floor. There were no other marks. The ceiling, too, was completely dry.

"There's nothing else wet around," he said. "Pete is right. Something was standing here. Something that left wet marks."

"Marks that big? They must be two or three feet long!" Bob said.

"At least," Jupiter said solemnly. "Big and wet and shiny. Sort of a——"

"Monster!" Pete finished the sentence for Jupiter.

"The Old One!" Bob exclaimed.

The three boys looked at each other nervously. They did not believe in unknown monsters, but what could have made such big, wet marks?

Then a powerful glare of light fixed the three boys like moths against the wall. A harsh voice called from behind the dazzling light.

"What's goin' on here?"

A figure came slowly toward them—a bent, twisted figure with a wild white beard, carrying an enormous-looking rifle.

6.
A Dangerous Passage

The old man pointed toward the dark tunnels that led from the cavern.

"Them passages goes a far piece inside," he said in a high, cracked voice. "You young'uns could get lost mighty easy in there."

The old man's red-rimmed eyes gleamed wickedly.

"Got to be mightly careful here," he croaked. "Got to know the country, yessir. Seventy years I lived out here, never lost my scalp. No sir. Got to think ahead, that's the story. Know the country and fight the enemy."

"Scalp?" Pete stared. "You fought Indians? Here?"

The old man waved his ancient rifle. "Injuns! I'll tell you about Injuns, I will. Lived with Injuns all my life. Fine people but hard enemies, yessir. Almost lost my scalp twice. Ute country and Apache country. Sneaky, the Apaches. But I got away."

"I don't think there are any Indians now, sir," Jupiter said politely, "and we won't become lost."

The old man's eyes suddenly focused on the boys. For the first time he actually seemed to be seeing them. "Now?" he repeated. "Of course there're no Injuns now. Are you boys crazy? You must be, wandering around in this cave. Strangers around here, eh?" His voice was lower now, and steadier, and he had lost his wild look.

Bob was the first to reply. "Yes sir, we're from Rocky Beach."

"We're staying at The Crooked-Y with Mr. and Mrs. Dalton," Jupiter explained. "Mr. . . . ?"

"Ben Jackson. You boys can call me Ben," the old man said. "The Daltons, eh? Fine people, yessiree. I was passing this old cave and thought I heard someone yell out. Guess that was one of you, eh?"

"Yes sir," Jupiter said, "but we weren't lost. You see, we mark our way so we always know how to get back."

"Blaze a trail, eh? Well now, that's mighty smart. I reckon maybe you would have been okay out in the big country in the old days. What are you doing in here, anyway?"

"We're trying to find out what makes the moaning sound," Bob explained.

"Only it stopped as soon as we came in," Pete added.

Suddenly the old man seemed to crouch. His eyes clouded again, and grew wary. The change was so startling that for a moment the boys could almost imagine they were looking at a different person.

"Moanin', eh?" Ben's voice was high-pitched again. "Folks say it's El Diablo come back. Not me, no sir. I say it's The Old One, that's what I say.

"The Old One lived in this here cave long before any white man showed up," he went on. "Time don't mean anything to The Old One. You boys stay out of here or The Old One'll get you sure. Jess Dalton, he better stay out, too. The sheriff, all of them. The Old One'll get them all!"

The old man's voice crackled in the dark shadows of the cavern. Bob and Pete looked nervously at Jupiter, who was watching old Ben intently.

"Have you ever seen him, Mr. Jackson?" Jupiter asked. "The Old One, I mean? Have you seen him here in the cave?"

"Seen him?" the old man cackled. "I seen something, yessir. More'n once I seen it."

The old man looked around warily, and then once again he changed. His twisted body straightened, his eyes cleared, his voice lowered and became calm.

"Well, you boys better come on out with me now. Can't leave you yelling in here, eh?"

Jupiter nodded. "I think we've seen enough for now anyway. You're quite right, it does seem easy to become lost in here."

The old man picked up his electric lantern. Its bright light made the shadows of the cave seem far less menacing.

They soon found their way out into the quiet valley. As the old man walked them to their bikes, Jupiter cocked his ear toward the cave to listen. But the moaning sound did not come again. They thanked Ben Jackson for coming in to find them and said good night.

"You're smart boys, yessir," the old man said. "Only The Old One's smarter than anyone. You boys better be careful. You tell Jess Dalton, The Old One is watching, yessir."

The old man's cackling laughter followed the boys as they rode down the dirt road in the moonlight. Rounding a curve, Jupiter suddenly stopped his bike.

"Oooff!" Pete grunted, narrowly missing him.

Bob stepped on his brakes. "What's wrong, Jupe?" he asked.

"The Three Investigators do not give up until a job is completed," Jupiter said, his bike already turned around and headed back the way they had come.

"I think we should go back to the ranch," Bob said.

"So do I," Pete added quickly.

"Two to one, Jupe," Bob pointed out.

But Jupiter had already started pedaling back the way they had come. Bob and Pete watched for a moment, then began to follow him. They both knew there was no stopping Jupiter once he had an idea in his head.

When they caught up with The First Investigator, he was peering cautiously around the curve in the dark road.

"It's all clear," Jupiter said. "Come on."

"What are we doing, Jupe?" Bob asked as The First Investigator got off his bike.

"We're going to leave the bikes here and walk," Jupiter explained. "We'll try to keep out of sight."

"Where do we walk to?" Pete wanted to know.

"I noticed that this road curves around Devil Mountain toward the sea," Jupiter explained. "I want to see if there is another entrance on the ocean side."

Bob and Pete followed Jupiter down the dark road. The valley was shadowy in the moonlight. Shapes seemed to loom up out of the night as they walked—trees and boulders and dark gullies.

"There are three puzzles that have come to our attention tonight," Jupiter said as they walked. "First, why did the moaning stop when we were inside the cave? I noticed that the wind was still blowing when we came out, so it wasn't the wind that changed."

"You mean something else made the moaning stop?" Bob asked.

"I'm sure of it," Jupiter said firmly.

"But what?" demanded Pete.

"Perhaps something or someone who saw us." Jupe replied. "Second," he went on, "it seemed to me that Ben Jackson really wanted us to get out of that cave. I wonder why?"

"The way he changed was spooky," Bob said, and he shivered, as if to prove it.

"Yes," Jupiter mused, "he is a most peculiar old man. It almost seemed as if he was two different people living in two different times. In fact, I couldn't help feeling that he was putting on some kind of performance."

"Maybe he was really worried about us, Jupe," Pete said. "I mean, if he really has seen . . . The Old One."

"Perhaps," Jupiter agreed. "And that's our third problem—the black, shiny thing you saw, and those marks on the cave floor. I'm sure they were water marks. Of course there may be a pool in the cave, but it's also possible that there's another entrance to the cave on the ocean side. And that is what we're going to look for!"

After the boys had walked a little farther, the road ended abruptly at an iron gate. Beyond it, two narrow paths, one to the left and one to the right, led down the rocky cliff. Far below, a white line of surf glowed in the moonlight. The boys climbed the fence and looked down over the steep cliff.

"We'll go to the right, toward the cave," Jupe said. "Pete had better lead and I'll come last. We'll rope ourselves together the way mountain climbers do. Then if we come to any difficult places, we'll cross them one at a time."

The boys quickly roped themselves together at their waists, and Pete led the way down the narrow path. Below, the sea surged in and out among giant black rocks made silvery by the moonlight. At low points on the path, spray flew up to drench the boys. Three times they had to turn and face the cliff to inch across narrow ledges.

At last the path led sharply downward and they found themselves on a small white-sand beach. The beach was deserted now, but there was considerable evidence that people had been swimming there— empty beer cans, soft-drink bottles, and the remains of picnic lunches.

"We'll look all along the cliff for some form of opening," Jupiter decided.

The cliff face was heavily overgrown with scrubby bushes and stunted trees, and hidden in many places by large boulders. With their lights the boys searched behind the bushes and boulders. But they found no entrance to the cave.

"I think we're looking in the wrong place, Jupe," Pete said.

"Where else is there to look?" Bob asked.

"Well," Pete explained, "no one has told us about another entrance. If there is one, I'll bet it's hard to get to."

"You mean it's not here on the beach?" Bob asked. "But it has to be near here because that path is the only way down."

"I think you're right," Jupiter said. "Bob, you come with me. We'll search on the right side. Pete, you go left."

The rocks bordering the beach were slippery with seaweed and mussels so Jupiter and Bob had to pick their way cautiously. Jupiter kept his flashlight aimed at the cliff face in order to look for an opening.

Finally, they reached a point where they could go no farther unless they plunged into the water. Discouraged, they were turning back when they heard Pete shout.

"I found it!"

Bob and Jupiter scrambled over the wet rocks and ran pell-mell down the beach. At the far end, Pete was standing on a big flat rock. Between two giant boulders, they saw an opening in the cliff face. It was a small opening, and only a foot above the sea.

"I can hear the moaning again," Pete said. "Listen."

There was no mistaking the sound.

"*Aaaaaaahhhhhhh—oooooooooooo—oooooo—ooo!*"

It floated out of the opening, very faint as if from deep inside the cavern.

Pete shown his flashlight into the entrance. It was black, wet and very narrow. The tunnel seemed to bore directly into the cliff face as far as they could see.

7.
Sounds in the Night

"It's awful narrow and dark, Jupe," Pete said uneasily.

"Maybe it doesn't go anywhere," Bob speculated.

"No," insisted Jupiter. "It must go into the cave or we wouldn't hear the moaning."

"It sure looks small," Pete said doubtfully.

Jupiter squatted and peered into the opening. "I think we can enter safely if we're careful. Bob, you're the smallest so we'll tie the rope to you and you'll go in first."

"Me? All alone? I thought we were all going to go in together."

"That would be the wrong way to do it, Bob,"

Jupiter explained. "When entering an unknown passage, the correct way is to send one person in, with a rope on him, while the other two remain outside ready to pull him out instantly if he encounters any danger."

"Sure," Pete added. "In those prison-camp movies, when the soldiers dug tunnels to escape, they always tied a rope to the man who was inside the tunnel. If he pulled once on the rope they hauled him out."

"Exactly," Jupiter said with a trace of annoyance. The First Investigator did not like to have anyone suggest that his ideas were not original. He turned to Bob. "Remember, pull hard on the rope if you get into any trouble. We'll pull you out."

Somewhat unconvinced but game, Bob tied the rope firmly around his waist. Cautiously he crawled into the narrow tunnel.

Inside it was dark and cold. The ceiling was much too low for him to stand up, and the walls were wet and slimy with green sea moss. He had to inch along on his hands and knees. As he crawled slowly forward, beaming his flashlight ahead, crabs scuttled away, their claws scraping on the damp rock.

After Bob had gone about thirty feet, the ceiling suddenly inclined sharply upward. He stood up. His flashlight beam showed that the tunnel still led straight ahead, but it had become wide and dry, and angled upward.

"Jupe! Pete! It's okay," he called back into the tunnel.

Soon both Pete and Jupiter were standing beside him.

"It's all dry here," Pete observed.

"This part must be above the high-tide mark," Jupiter said. "I'll start marking our trail, and you and Bob listen for the moaning so we can go in the right direction."

They moved ahead, Jupiter stopping every ten feet or so to leave question marks in white chalk. After some forty feet they emerged into still another of the vast caverns that seemed to honeycomb the interior of Devil Mountain. Once more many dark passages led out of the large room.

The boys looked at each other in dismay.

"Well, here we go again," Pete said.

"This mountain is nothing but tunnels." Bob sounded discouraged. "How will we ever trace the sound?"

But Jupiter was not really looking at the new cavern or the many tunnel exits. He was listening.

"Have either of you heard the moaning since we came in?" Jupe asked.

Bob and Pete looked at each other.

"Gosh, no," Bob said.

"Not since we were outside!" Pete agreed.

"I didn't hear it all the time I was crawling," Bob added.

Jupiter nodded thoughtfully. "As soon as we enter, the moaning stops. A most suspicious circumstance. Not once, which could be an accident, but twice now."

Pete was puzzled. "You think maybe we do something when we come in? I mean, maybe we change something without knowing we change it?"

"That's one possibility," Jupiter acknowledged.

"Another explanation might be that someone sees us." said Bob. "But how could anyone have seen us on that beach in the dark?"

Jupiter shook his head. "I admit I'm at a loss to explain it myself. Perhaps it is just——"

They all heard the sound at the same moment. A faint and distant jingling of bells, and the *clip-clop, clip-clop* of a horse's hoofs.

"A horse!" Bob exclaimed.

Jupiter turned his head and listened intently. The sound seemed to come from the wall of the cavern.

"It's . . . inside the mountain!" Jupiter said.

Bob protested. "It can't be, Jupe. It has to be from another part of the cave."

Jupiter shook his head. "If my sense of direction is correct, the other part of the cave is to our left," he said. "We are facing the side of the mountain—and no tunnels go in that direction!"

"Maybe we better get out," Pete suggested.

"I think," Jupiter said hurriedly, "Pete is right. Let's go!"

The boys pushed pell-mell against each other in

their scramble for the narrow exit. Pete reached the small tunnel first and began to crawl through. Jupiter and Bob followed right behind.

They tumbled out into water up to their knees, and floundered across the flat rocks till they sprawled at last on the white sand of the beach. They lay there panting.

"Where *did* that noise come from?" Bob finally broke the silence.

"I don't know," Jupiter admitted reluctantly. "But I think we've done enough exploring for one night. Let's start back."

Bob and Pete were only too glad to follow the First Investigator back up the narrow trail. They had nearly reached the iron gate at the top of the cliff when Jupiter suddenly stopped. In the darkness Pete almost ran into him.

"What are you doing, Jupe!"

Jupiter didn't reply. He was staring up at the twin peaks of Devil Mountain.

"What is it?" Bob asked in a whisper.

"I just had an idea," Jupiter answered slowly. "And I also thought I saw something move up there on the mountain where——"

The sound of jingling carried across the night along with the *clip-clop, clip-clop, clip-clop* of horse's hoofs.

"Oh no!" Bob groaned.

"Is that what we heard inside the cave?" whispered Pete.

"I think so," Jupiter said. "The sound must have

filtered down through some crevice in the rock of the mountain. Sound carries very clearly that way. It would have seemed as if it was inside the mountain itself."

The boys crouched down in the thick bushes near the gate as the hoofbeats came closer. Then a great black horse appeared on the steep slopes of Devil Mountain. It came down the mountain at a trot and passed within a few feet from where the boys crouched in the bushes.

"There's no rider!" Bob whispered.

"Should we try to catch it?" asked Pete.

"No, I don't think so," Jupiter replied. "Let's wait."

The boys crouched silently under cover of the bushes. Suddenly Pete stiffened, and pointed toward the slope. A man was coming down the mountain at a fast walk. As he passed their hiding place, they had a clear view of him in the moonlight. He was a tall, dark man with a long nose, a ragged scar on his right cheek, and a black patch over his right eye!

"Did you see that eye patch?" hissed Pete.

"And the scar," Bob added.

"I was more interested in his suit," Jupiter whispered. "It was definitely a business suit, and unless I am mistaken I think he had a pistol under his coat!"

"Can't we go now, Jupe?" said Pete nervously.

"Yes, I think we'd better," Jupiter agreed. "This has been a most interesting night."

Pete and Bob needed no urging. As they hurried along the road to where they had left their bikes, they kept looking behind them anxiously. But they saw nothing else. While they were riding past the end of Moaning Valley, however, a long wail echoed through the night.

"*Aaaaaaaaaaaahhhhhhhhh—ooooooooooooooooo —oooooo—ooo!*"

The boys began to pedal furiously in the direction of the ranch house.

8.
El Diablo!

Pete woke up in bright sunlight. Confused, he looked around the unfamiliar room. Where was he? Then a horse whinnied somewhere outside, a cow lowed, and Pete remembered that he was in the upstairs bedroom of The Crooked-Y. He leaned over the edge of his top bunk to see what Jupiter was up to. Jupiter was not there.

Pete sat up quickly, bumping his head on the low ceiling.

"Ouch!" he grunted.

"Shhhhhh!" Bob hissed from his bunk across the room, and pointed toward the window.

In front of the window Jupiter sat cross-legged on the floor, looking like a small Buddha in his bathrobe. A large sheet of paper was spread out on the

58

floor in front of him and in the middle of it he had stacked four books. On the paper Jupiter had drawn a lot of pencil lines.

As Pete stared down at the books and the paper and the pencil marks he realized that Jupiter had made a rough model of Moaning Valley. He had marked the cave entrances in pencil.

"He's been sitting like that for an hour," Bob explained.

"Gosh," Pete said. "I couldn't sit like that for ten minutes!" The intense concentration of their stocky friend always awed Bob and Pete.

Suddenly, Jupiter spoke. "I am ascertaining the exact topographical arrangement of Moaning Valley, Pete. The key to our puzzle lies in the physical pattern."

"Huh?" Pete said.

"Jupe means that he thinks the mystery can be solved by studying the lay of the land," Bob explained.

"Oh," Pete said. "Why didn't he say so?"

Ignoring Pete, Jupiter went on, "The real mystery of Moaning Valley is why does the moaning stop when we go inside? It happened twice last night, yet when we were leaving the area the moaning began again."

He held up a newspaper. "I have here a newspaper report of the sudden recurrence of the moaning. In it the sheriff says that the main reason no one has been able to identify the cause of the moaning is that once inside they never hear it anymore."

Jupiter put down the paper. "I'm convinced now that the moaning doesn't stop by accident!"

"I guess you're right," Bob said. "The way it started again right when we were leaving sure looks like someone was watching us."

"But how does that—uh—model help us, Jupe?" Pete blurted out.

Jupiter looked down at his crude model. "I've marked all the places we were last night. Now we know that both times we entered the cave the moaning stopped instantly. It happened too quickly for it to have been someone *inside* the cave who was watching us."

Bob nodded eagerly. "I get it! So we had to be seen *before* we went in."

"Exactly," Jupiter said, "and from my model I've deduced that we could have been seen everywhere we went from only one place—the top of Devil Mountain."

"Then all we have to do is tell Mr. Dalton someone is up on Devil Mountain and let him catch the person!" exclaimed Pete.

Jupiter shook his head. "No, Pete, no one would believe us unless they caught the man, and it would be almost impossible to get to the top without being seen. Whoever is up there would just run away."

"Then——" Bob began.

"How——" Pete started at the same instant.

"We will have to observe what is actually happening in the cave," Jupiter said solemnly, "so that we can tell people the full story."

"But we don't know what's happening in the cave," Pete objected. "Do we?"

"No, but I've got a plan in mind," revealed Jupiter, "And I've got a clue as to what it's all about!"

"You do?" Pete said. "What is it?"

"Last night I found this in one of the passages," Jupiter explained, holding up the rough, blackish stone he had found in the mine-shaft passage. "The passage was once a mine shaft, and I found this stone just where it ended in one of those blockages."

Bob took the little stone, looked at it with a puzzled expression and passed it on to Pete.

"But what is it, Jupe?" Pete demanded. "I mean, besides a kind of hard, slippery stone?"

"Scratch the window with it," Jupiter said.

"What?" Pete said, surprised. "You know it won't——"

"Go ahead," Jupiter urged, a smug expression on his round face.

Pete went to the window and scratched the small stone over the glass. It cut into the glass almost as easily as a knife cutting into butter. Pete let out a low whistle.

"Jupe!" Bob exclaimed. "You mean that's a——"

"Diamond," Jupiter finished. "Yes, I think that's exactly what it is. A rough, uncut diamond.

And a pretty big one. I think its quality isn't good, probably no more than an industrial stone. But it is a diamond."

"You mean El Diablo's Cave is a diamond mine? Here in California?" Bob asked skeptically.

"Well, there have been rumors, I think, and——"

That was as far as he got. A vigorous knock on the bedroom door interrupted him, and Mrs. Dalton's voice called, "Up and at 'em, boys! Breakfast's on the table. We'll have no late sleeping here!"

Everything else was forgotten for the moment as the boys realized how hungry they were. They dressed and were in the big ranch kitchen five minutes later. Mr. Dalton and Professor Walsh smiled at them.

"Well, I see that Moaning Valley and its mystery have not affected your appetites, boys," Professor Walsh commented.

Mrs. Dalton bustled around the roomy, bright kitchen and soon the boys were digging into stacks of buckwheat cakes and ham, and drinking mugs of cold fresh milk.

"You boys ready to do some work today?" Mr. Dalton asked.

"Of course they are," Mrs. Dalton said. "Why not take them up to the north meadow for the haying?"

"Good idea," Mr. Dalton agreed. "Later they

can help round up some mavericks."

The boys, who had done some reading on ranch life, knew that "mavericks" were cattle that had strayed from the main herd into remote parts of the range.

"Did you boys have a good walk on the beach last night?" Professor Walsh asked. "What did you find?"

"We had an interesting expedition," Jupiter answered. "And we met a rather odd old man. He called himself Ben Jackson. Who is he, sir?"

"Old Ben and his partner, Waldo Turner, are prospectors," Mr. Dalton explained. "I imagine they've looked for gold and silver and precious stones all over the West in their day."

"According to local gossip they came here many years ago," Mrs. Dalton added, "when there was a rumor that gold had been found. Of course, there never was any gold, but apparently Old Ben and Waldo never gave up. They have a shack on our land, and still consider themselves prospectors. They don't seem to like to have visitors, but they don't mind getting handouts from the ranchers around here. Of course, we call it a grubstake. They wouldn't take charity."

"They're quite famous local characters," Professor Walsh put in.

"They can really tell you stories." Mr. Dalton smiled. "Of course, they're somewhat eccentric, and most of their stories are just tall tales. For example, they'll tell you about fighting the Indians, but I doubt if they ever did."

"Gosh, you mean all that was a lie?" Pete exclaimed.

Before Mr. Dalton could reply, the back door of the kitchen burst open. The foreman, Luke Hardin, came in hurriedly.

"They just found young Castro out in Moanin' Valley," Hardin said grimly.

"Castro?" Mr. Dalton looked worried.

"Got thrown from his horse last night while he was riding herd on some strays. Lay there all night," said Hardin.

"Is he all right?" Mrs. Dalton asked.

"Doc says he's okay. They took him over to the hospital in Santa Carla."

"I'll go and see him right away!" Mr. Dalton jumped up.

"The men are kind of shook up," Hardin added, his face dark. "Two more told me they're going to quit. Castro was out in Moanin' Valley and says he saw something moving. He took a look. Whatever it was spooked his horse. He was thrown and the horse ran off. He's all bruised up and his ankle's sprained."

The Daltons looked at each other in despair. Jupiter spoke up.

"Was his horse a big black one, Mr. Hardin?" he asked.

"That's right—Big Ebony. A good horse. Came back to the corral on his own this morning, so we knew to look for young Castro."

Mr. Dalton spoke sharply. "Did you boys see Big Ebony last night?"

"Yes sir," Jupiter said. "A big black horse without a rider."

"You must always report a riderless horse on a ranch, boys," Mr. Dalton said severely. "We would have found Castro sooner."

"We would have, sir," Jupe explained, "but we saw a man following him and assumed that he was the rider. He was a tall man, with a scar on his right cheek and an eye patch."

Mr. Dalton shook his head. "Never heard of a man like that."

"Tall and an eye patch?" Professor Walsh inquired. "Sounds menacing, but definitely not El Diablo, eh? He wasn't tall, and he didn't wear an eye patch."

Mr. Dalton started for the door. "Luke, get the men calmed down if you can. I'll join you in the north meadow after I see Castro. And I think I'll talk to the sheriff about that man the boys say they saw."

Jupiter spoke up again. "If you're going into town, sir, perhaps you would take me? I have to return to Rocky Beach today."

"Why, Jupiter, you're not leaving us?" Mrs. Dalton asked.

"Oh, no," Jupiter assured her. "It's only that we need our scuba equipment. We saw some reefs off shore last night which look excellent for collecting specimens for our marine biology studies."

Bob and Pete stared at Jupe. They did not remember that they had seen any reefs, or that they were conducting marine biology studies. But they said nothing. They had learned not to question Jupiter when he had some scheme in mind.

"I'm afraid I don't have time today to take you down," Mr. Dalton said, "and I can't spare a man or a truck. You'd better wait a few days."

"That's quite all right, sir," Jupiter said. "If you'll take me into town I'll get the bus down. Someone will drive me back."

"Better hurry up and get ready, then," Mr. Dalton told him as he went out the door.

Mrs. Dalton looked at Bob and Pete. "I'm afraid you boys had better find something to do, too. With this trouble, Mr. Dalton won't have time to work with you today."

"We will, ma'am," Bob assured her.

The boys went back to their room while Jupiter gathered what he needed for his return to Rocky Beach. As he packed, he revealed what he had in mind for Bob and Pete while he was gone.

"I want you to go into Santa Carla and buy a dozen large, plain candles," Jupe said, "and three Mexican sombreros. With the Fiesta in Santa Carla there should be plenty of hats to buy. Tell Mr. and

Mrs. Dalton you are going in to see the Fiesta parade."

"Three sombreros?" Pete repeated.

"Right," said Jupiter, without further explanation. "Then go to the library. Bob, I want you to learn all you can about the history of Devil Mountain and Moaning Valley. I mean all the exact details, not just the legends."

"I'll find out all I can," Bob assured the First Investigator. "What are you *really* going to Rocky Beach for?"

"To get the scuba equipment, as I said," Jupiter replied, "and to take the diamond into Los Angeles to have it examined by an expert."

Mr. Dalton called from below. "Jupiter! Ready?"

The boys hurried down, and Jupiter climbed into the cab of the pick-up truck. As Bob and Pete watched him ride off, they realized that they still didn't know what Jupe was planning to do with the scuba equipment.

After helping Mrs. Dalton in the kitchen for an hour or so, Bob borrowed Mrs. Dalton's library card, and the two boys started off for Santa Carla on their bicycles.

"Enjoy the Fiesta, boys!" Mrs. Dalton called after them.

Actually, Bob and Pete were quite excited at the prospect of seeing the famous Santa Carla Fiesta, and they rode off in a holiday mood. The road from the ranch wound through the vast inland valley, surrounded on three sides by the brown mountains of Southern California. Away from the sea the sun was hot, and the boys noticed that all the creeks they passed were dry. At one point they crossed the wide bed of the Santa Carla River itself. Down below the bridge, the river bed was completely dried up, with small plants growing on its sun-baked surface.

Soon the highway began to climb toward San Mateo Pass. Bob and Pete had to get off their bikes and walk them around hairpin curves. Mountain valleys yawned close to the right, while rocky cliffs climbed steeply to the left. The boys walked slowly in the bright sun. After a long, hot hike they finally emerged at the top of the pass.

"Golly! Look at that!" Pete cried.

"Wow!" exclaimed Bob almost at the same moment.

Spread out before their eyes was a breath-taking panorama. The mountains sloped away to low foothills and then a wide coastal plain that spread in all directions to the blue water of the Pacific Ocean. The city of Santa Carla shimmered in the sun, its houses like tiny boxes in the great green expanse. Boats moved on the blue surface of the sea, and the mountainous Channel Islands seemed to float in the distance.

The boys were still staring at the magnificent sight when they heard thundering hoofbeats behind them. They whirled to see a horseman galloping down the highway straight at them. He rode a great black horse with a silver-mounted bridle and a silver-trimmed *charro* saddle, its enormous pommel horn glinting in the sun.

The boys stood transfixed as the horse bore down on them. The rider was a small, slender man with dark eyes who wore a black sombrero, a short black jacket, flared trousers, and a black bandanna over the lower half of his face. He carried an ancient pistol that was aimed straight at the boys.

El Diablo!

9.
A Sudden Attack

The black horse reared high above the paralyzed boys, its hoofs pawing wildly at the air.

The rider waved his pistol and shouted, "Viva Fiesta!" Then he slipped off his black bandanna to reveal a boyish face full of mischief.

"Come on to the Fiesta!" the young man shouted again, turned his horse in mid-air, and galloped off down the highway toward Santa Carla.

The boys stared after him.

"A Fiesta costume!" Pete groaned.

They looked at each other and laughed with relief. Scared by a boy in costume!

"I'll bet there are ten El Diablos in the Fiesta," Bob observed.

"Well, I hope we don't run into any of them in dark alleys," Pete said.

The boys climbed back on their bikes and began the long descent down the winding pass road. Soon they came out of the mountains into the outskirts of Santa Carla. They rode past housing tracts, a golf course and several outlying shopping centers of the bustling resort city.

When they reached the downtown section, they parked their bikes in a rack at the library and walked to Union Street, the main thoroughfare of Santa Carla. The street was blocked by police barriers in preparation for the Fiesta parade. People were already lined up behind the barriers, most of them dressed in the colorful costumes of old Spanish days. A holiday atmosphere filled the air.

Bob and Pete hurried to make their purchases at a little shop selling souvenirs. They bought a dozen thick white candles and three straw sombreros. Then they rushed out to the curb just as the first band came marching past with a blare of trumpets and banging of drums.

After the band came the floats, decked with flowers and pretty girls and men in costumes. Most depicted important moments of California history. One showed Father Junipéro Serra, the Franciscan missionary who had established most of the fine old missions that stretched up the long coast of California. Another represented the day John C. Fremont had raised the American flag over Santa Carla when the city had been taken from Mexico. Another showed El Diablo in his famous escape. At least five El Diablos rode around this float. One of them was the same grinning young rider on the black horse who had startled them at the top of the pass.

"Look at all the horses!" exclaimed Bob.

"I sure wish I could ride like that." Pete watched the horsemen with admiration.

Both boys were good riders, though not yet perfect, and they watched the horses with great interest. Ranchers in Spanish costumes, along with mounted police posses from up and down the state, went by, riding troops of golden palominos. Some of the horses performed intricate dance steps out in the street.

There were carriages and covered wagons and old stagecoaches, and then a float depicting Gold Rush days. Bob shook Pete's arm.

"Look!" he whispered, pointing toward two men who were walking beside the Gold Rush float. They had a burro loaded with food and shovels and pickaxes, and one of them was the bearded old man from the cave—Ben Jackson.

"The other one must be his partner, Waldo Turner," Bob said.

The two old-timers seemed to delight the crowd. They looked like real prospectors, even to the dust and dirt on their mining clothes. Old Ben was obviously the leader, his white beard flowing as he limped proudly along, leading the burro. Waldo

Turner, a taller and thinner old man with a white mustache instead of a beard, followed behind.

The floats kept coming, the bands played on, and the boys might have forgotten all about their mission at the library if Pete hadn't suddenly noticed the man.

"Bob!" he whispered urgently.

Bob looked up and there, a few feet away, was the tall, scar-faced man with the eye patch. The man didn't seem at all interested in the parade. As the boys watched, he hurried across Union Street and vanished.

"Come on," Bob said, and the boys quickly followed.

At the corner, they saw the tall man some twenty feet ahead and walking fast. From time to time he slowed down, as if watching something ahead.

"I think he's following someone," Bob observed.

"Can you see who it is?" asked Pete.

"No, you're taller," Bob said.

Pete stood as tall as he could, but he couldn't tell who or what the man was following. Then he saw him turn off the sidewalk.

"He's going into a building," Pete reported.

"It's the library!" said Bob.

The man vanished through the tall double doors, and the boys hurried after him. Inside, they stopped. The library was almost deserted on this Fiesta day, yet the boys could see no trace of the tall man with the eye patch.

The main room was large, with many book stacks and several exits into other rooms. Quickly the boys looked up and down the aisles between the stacks. Then they explored the exits. To their dismay they found that the library had two doors leading to a side street. And the tall man was nowhere in sight.

"He's gone," Pete said, crestfallen.

"We should have split up and one of us gone around to the back. Jupiter would have remembered that most libraries have more than one entrance," Bob said dejectedly. He was unhappy with himself for not thinking of such an obvious point.

"Well," Pete said. "He's gone and we might as well get on with that research Jupe wanted."

Bob agreed, and the two boys inquired about where they would find books on local history. A kindly librarian directed them to a small room that contained a special California history collection. Just as they were walking up to the desk in the smaller room, a heavy hand fell on Pete's shoulder.

"Well, well, our young investigators!"

Professor Walsh stood behind them, his eyes twinkling behind his thick glasses.

"Doing some research, boys?" he asked.

"Yes sir," replied Pete. "We want to find out all about Moaning Valley."

"Good, good," Professor Walsh said encouragingly. "That's just what I'm doing myself. I haven't had a great deal of luck, though. There doesn't seem to be much except unreliable legends. . . . Have you been to the Fiesta?"

"Yes sir," Pete replied enthusiastically. "Boy, they sure have some great horses."

"It's a fine celebration," the professor agreed. "I think I'll go take a look since I'm not having much luck here. How are you boys going to get back to the ranch?"

"We have our bikes, sir," Bob said.

"Well, then, I'll see you later." Professor Walsh turned to leave.

Bob hesitated, then asked, "Did you happen to see a tall man with an eye patch while you were in the library?"

Walsh shook his head. "No, boys, I didn't. You mean that same man you saw last night?"

"Yes, sir," Pete said.

"Right here in town, eh?" Professor Walsh looked thoughtful. "No, I haven't seen him."

After the professor had gone, Bob and Pete went to work. They found three or four books that mentioned Moaning Valley, but none of them added anything to what they already knew. Then Bob discovered a small book, with yellowing, wrinkled pages, which was a complete history of Moaning Valley up to the year 1941. It was on the wrong shelf, which was probably the reason Professor Walsh hadn't seen it.

They checked the book out on Mrs. Dalton's library card. Outside, the afternoon was still hot and sunny and the parade was just ending. People were streaming away from the main part of town, many of them still in costume. The boys tied their packages on the luggage racks of their bikes and started home. Soon they began the long climb up San Mateo Pass. They rode as far up as they could with ease, then dismounted and continued on foot.

Stopping to rest a moment, they looked out over the water toward the Channel Islands, hazy in the distance.

"Gosh, I'd like to get out to those islands," Pete said.

"They actually herd cattle on some of them," Bob said. "Cowboys and all, right out in the ocean."

Near the islands they could see the slim gray hulls of Navy vessels on maneuvers.

A car was coming up the highway from the direction of Santa Carla, but the boys were busy gazing out at the ocean. They paid no attention to the car until they suddenly realized, from the rasp of the motor, that it was traveling at top speed.

Whirling around, they discovered that it was partly off the road and heading straight for them.

"Look out, Bob!" Pete shouted.

Both boys leaped out of the path of the onrushing car just in time. It roared past them, veered back onto the road and raced away.

But their desperate leaps had carried them over the edge of the road. Slipping, unable to hold on, they plunged toward the deep chasm far below.

10.
Jupiter Reveals
a Plan

Pete slid down the steep incline over sharp rocks and brush that tore at his clothes. He clawed at the bushes to slow his fall, for the slope ended in an almost sheer drop ahead. But the vegetation was not strong enough to hold him. He was only some four feet from empty space when he crashed into the heavy trunk of a twisted tree.

"Oof!" Pete grunted, as his fingers instinctively closed around the thick trunk.

For a moment he lay still, clinging to the tree trunk and breathing heavily. Then he realized that he was alone.

"Bob!" he cried.

There was no answer. Below him was nothing but yawning empty space.

"Bob!" he called again frantically.

There was movement just to Pete's left. Bob's face peered up through thick bushes.

"I'm all right . . . I guess," Bob said weakly. "I'm on a kind of ledge. Only . . . I can't move my leg!"

"Try moving it just a little."

Pete waited while he saw faint movement in the bushes where Bob lay. Then Bob's voice came more strongly.

"I don't think it's bad," Bob reported. "I can move it. It was just twisted under me. It hurts, but not so much."

"Do you think you can crawl back up?" Pete asked after a minute.

"I don't know, Pete. It's awful steep."

"And if we slip——" Pete did not have to finish that statement.

"I guess we'd better try yelling," Bob said.

"Loud," agreed Pete.

He opened his mouth to yell, but what came out was only a faint whisper. For just as he started to shout he spied a long face peering down from the edge of the road above. A face with a wicked scar and an eye patch!

The boys and the man with the scarred face stared at each other for a full ten seconds. Then, abruptly, the face vanished and they heard the sound of running feet, a car engine, and the squeal of tires as the car roared away.

Its motor had scarcely faded out of hearing when the boys heard other vehicles approaching.

"Yell!" Pete cried.

Both boys shouted as loud as they could, and the sound echoed through the mountains. Brakes squealed and gravel crunched above. Two kindly faces peered over the edge of the road.

Soon a thick rope came flying down to Pete. He wrapped it twice around his waist, held the loose end in both hands, and was pulled up to the road. The rope was thrown down again, and a moment later Bob stood beside Pete.

Bob tested his leg and decided it was probably only sprained. The burly truck driver who had supplied the rope was going in the direction of The Crooked-Y, and he insisted that the boys accept a ride with him. Less than fifteen minutes later they were deposited with their bikes at the front gate of the ranch. They waved their thanks to the truck driver, and limped up to the porch of the ranch house.

Mrs. Dalton came out of the house and stared at them. "Good heavens! What happened? Your clothes are a sight!"

Pete started to answer when he felt a light kick from Bob.

"We went downhill too fast and fell off our bikes in the pass, ma'am," Bob explained, which was more or less true. "I hurt my leg a little, so a man gave us a ride."

"Your leg?" Mrs. Dalton said. "Let me see, Bob."

Like most ranch women Mrs. Dalton was a good practical nurse. She pronounced Bob's leg uninjured except for a mild sprain. No doctor would be needed, but Bob would have to rest his leg as much as possible. Mrs. Dalton sat him on the porch in a comfortable chair and brought him a pitcher of lemonade.

"But you can get to work, Pete Crenshaw," she said. "Mr. Dalton isn't back yet so you can start by haying the horses in the front corral."

"Yes, ma'am," Pete said hastily.

Bob sat in the shade with his leg up on a chair and grinned while his friend worked in the hot sun. Pete glared at the smaller boy, but he didn't really mind. It felt good to be working with his muscles in the warm sun.

Just before suppertime Jupiter pulled up in the truck from his uncle's salvage yard with big, blond Konrad at the wheel. Pete helped Jupiter unload the scuba equipment and store it in the barn, along with another small, mysterious bundle.

Konrad stayed for supper, and Mr. Dalton admired the enormous stature and muscles of Titus Jones's Bavarian helper.

"How would you like to work on a ranch, Konrad?" Mr. Dalton said. "If I had you with me, I could afford to lose ten hands."

"You need help, maybe for a few weeks," Konrad said, "Mr. Titus let Hans and me come to help, sure."

Mr. Dalton thanked him. "I hope it won't come to that. I'm sure this will all blow over soon. Young Castro says he isn't frightened, and he's going to talk to the men when he comes out of the hospital."

"That's wonderful, Jess," Mrs. Dalton said.

Mr. Dalton turned suddenly gloomy. "But I'm not sure there's time. The men may all be gone by then if these accidents continue. The sheriff hasn't come up with any ideas about Moaning Valley. He said El Diablo had no children he knows about, and he can't identify that man the boys saw."

"I'm sure an explanation will be found soon," Professor Walsh said encouragingly. "Reason will prevail over superstition as soon as the men start to think. Time—that is the healer."

"I wish I could be sure of that," Mr. Dalton said.

The adults started talking about other things, and when supper was over Konrad left to drive back to Rocky Beach. Professor Walsh had to deliver a lecture at the university, and the Daltons had to go over the ranch accounts. The boys went up to their room.

The instant they closed the door, Bob and Pete gathered around Jupiter.

"What's the plan?" Pete demanded.

"Was it a diamond?" Bob asked.

Jupiter grinned. "It's a diamond all right, just as I thought. A large industrial-type diamond, not worth much; but the expert in Los Angeles was most surprised when I told him where I discovered it. He found it pretty difficult to believe. He said he would have thought it was an African stone. I left it with him for various tests. He will call me here as soon as he completes his study."

"Wow!" Pete exclaimed.

"Did you get the candles and sombreros?" Jupiter asked.

"We sure did," Pete said.

"And a book about Moaning Valley," Bob added.

The two boys told Jupiter about their trip to Santa Carla and the car that had forced them off the road.

"Did you get the license number?" Jupiter asked immediately.

"Believe me, Jupe, there wasn't time," Pete said, "but I did notice that it was a different plate—sort of blue and white."

"Hmmmmm," Jupiter mused, "probably a Nevada plate. And you say the scar-faced man looked down at you?"

"Probably came back to finish the job, but the other cars scared him off," Pete said angrily.

"Perhaps," Jupiter said thoughtfully. "And you also saw the professor in town?"

"And Old Ben and his partner, Waldo," Bob pointed out.

"Of course the top of the pass is only a few

miles from here," Jupiter mused. "Anyone from the ranch or the valley could have driven up there in just a few minutes and probably not have been missed."

"Gee, I guess so," Bob agreed.

"Still," Jupiter went on thoughtfully, "a Nevada license plate is most interesting. As far as we know, no one around the ranch has anything but a California plate."

"You mean there's someone around here we don't know?" Pete said.

"Sure there is," Bob told him. "That man with the eye patch."

"It looks that way," Jupiter agreed, "but now we must get to work. I'll look through that book on Moaning Valley while you two go down and check the scuba equipment. Wrap the tanks in something that will disguise them, and then put them on the bikes with the candles, the sombreros and the bundle I brought."

"The plan!" Bob and Pete said together. "What is it?"

"I'll tell you on the way," Jupiter said, and looked at his prized chronometer. "We have to hurry now if we're going to reach Moaning Valley before sundown. Tonight we may solve the mystery of Moaning Valley!"

Half an hour later the First Investigator appeared in the barn, waving the book at Bob and Pete.

"I think I've found part of the answer," Jupiter

announced. "It says here that about fifty years ago they sealed up many of the old mine shafts in Devil Mountain. They had never found any gold or anything else, so they closed up the tunnels. Fifty years ago was when the original moaning sound stopped!"

"You mean one of them has been opened up again?" asked Bob. "And the wind blowing through it causes the moaning sound?"

"Yes, I think so," Jupiter agreed. "The question is how and why? . . . Are you fellows ready?"

"Ready, Jupe," Pete said.

"All right, then put on the sombreros before we ride out of the barn," Jupiter instructed.

The boys donned the wide-brimmed straw hats, balanced the heavy tanks disguised in burlap sacks, and mounted their bikes. The bikes proved somewhat hard to handle with the weight on them, and it was clear they would have to pedal with care.

"Ohhhh," Bob cried, wincing with pain.

"Is it your ankle, Bob?" asked Pete.

"It's all the weight on the bike," Jupiter decided.

Bob nodded unhappily. "I don't think I can make it, Jupe. I guess I'll have to stay behind."

Jupiter had his thoughtful look. "No, I don't think you have to stay behind, Bob. Perhaps we can turn this misfortune into an advantage. It will make our deception more convincing."

"What deception?" Pete asked, bewildered.

"The classic military tactic of the campfires and logs that look like cannon," Jupiter explained obscurely. "Bob, unload your scuba equipment. Without the weight I think you can operate the bike."

Bob tried again and found that without the extra weight he could indeed pedal satisfactorily. The boys rode out of the barn toward the gate. As they passed the house Mrs. Dalton waved from the porch.

"Have a good time, boys, and don't stay out too late!" she called. "And be careful!"

Once out of sight of the ranch, the boys pedaled faster toward Moaning Valley. When they reached the place where the road ended at the iron gate, they dismounted and carried their bundles and their bikes into the thick bushes.

"Now," Jupiter said, "here is my plan. We're going to get inside the cave without being seen."

Pete nodded. "I get it. We'll take the moaning by surprise."

"Right," said Jupe. "Of course, if my theory is correct we're being watched closely right now!"

"Gosh," Bob said, "then how do we do it?"

"We go under water," Jupiter told them, "using the scuba equipment. I checked on the tide and it's higher this evening. I estimate that most of the tunnel from the beach will be under water."

"But, Jupe," Bob objected, "how will we get into the water without being seen if we're being watched now?"

Jupiter beamed triumphantly. "We will use the decoy tactic. The way armies used to light campfires at night, and then slip away in the dark."

"But——" Pete began.

"You see," Jupiter went on, "I also noticed last

night that while the trail to the right is in clear view from the top of Devil Mountain, the trail to the left is hidden. Come on. Walk casually and in the open."

The three boys climbed over the iron gate and continued down the cliff path to the left. When they were just out of sight from the top of Devil Mountain, Jupiter said, "Stop here." The boys put down the scuba tanks, and watched as Jupiter opened the secret package.

"That's just old clothes!" exclaimed Pete.

"The same as those we're wearing!" Bob added.

"Exactly," said Jupiter. "Stuff them with brush, and tie off the arms and legs with this cord."

Bob and Pete did as Jupe said and in a few moments they had two dummies that looked remarkably like Pete and Jupiter.

"And the sombreros will hide our faces!" Pete said.

"Precisely," agreed Jupiter. "In addition they can be easily seen from the top of the mountain. Whoever is up there will be convinced that the dummies are us, especially since Bob will stay here with them and move from time to time!"

Quickly the boys set up the dummies above the trail. Bob sat beside the dummies, pretending to talk to them. From a distance it would look exactly as if The Three Investigators were sitting at the cliff edge observing the view.

Hidden below the cliff, Jupiter and Pete slipped down the trail to the small beach at the bottom. There they struggled into their air tanks.

"The surf is light tonight," Jupiter said. "We should have no trouble swimming from here to the cave entrance."

Pete nodded. "Underwater it shouldn't take more than five minutes to swim that far with our flippers."

"Right," Jupiter agreed. "I have my compass, and if necessary we can surface briefly. Our decoys should keep anyone from bothering to watch the ocean."

The boys fixed their breathing tubes in their mouths, walked backward into the water, and slid beneath the waves.

11.
Shadow Under the Sea

Pete followed Jupiter's waving fins through the bright, translucent water. Both boys were experienced scuba divers and swam only with their feet, with no wasted motion. Pete maintained a wary watch on the dark shadows of the rocks, while Jupiter concentrated on following the direction with his wrist compass.

Fish darted around them, and one large halibut, which had been invisible against the bottom, startled Pete by separating itself from the rocks and swimming majestically away.

After a couple of minutes, Jupiter stopped and turned to face Pete. He pointed to his diving chronometer and then toward the shore. Pete nodded. It was time to start in for El Diablo's Cave.

Jupiter continued to lead the way. Closer to shore the water was murky, and there were more rocks, so Pete swam closer to the flapping fins in front of him. In fact, he swam so close that he bumped hard into Jupiter's back when The First Investigator suddenly stopped.

Pete grunted, a little annoyed. His annoyance abruptly vanished as he saw that Jupiter was frantically pointing to the left. Pete looked.

A dark shape moved slowly through the water no more than thirty feet from them. It was large and long, like a big, black, hazy cigar—the shape of a shark or even a killer whale!

Pete's heart thudded. But the boys had been carefully instructed about what to do if they ran into a shark. They reacted to their training instantly. Moving as little as possible, since movement would attract a shark, they sank to the bottom. They drew their diving knives as a precaution, and began to edge their way slowly toward the safety of the rocks.

Pete watched the shape intently. He decided that it moved too steadily, too rigidly in a straight line, and was too long for a shark. At the same time, it seemed too small and slow for a killer whale.

Jupiter touched him on the shoulder and made the sign for a shark. Pete shook his head and both boys watched the strange shape slowly fade away out to sea. Then they swam in until the surge of the surf told them they were close to the cliff of Devil Mountain. They surfaced cautiously and found themselves only a few feet from the cave mouth.

"What was it?" Jupiter asked as soon as he removed his mouthpiece.

"I don't know," Pete replied nervously. "I'm pretty sure it wasn't a shark or whale or any kind of fish. Maybe we should go back, Jupe, and get the sheriff."

"If a whole posse came here they wouldn't find anything," Jupiter pointed out. "Whatever that shape was, it was going away, right? I'm sure that there is some simple explanation for it and, anyway, it's gone now."

"Well . . ." Pete hesitated.

"Now that we're this far, it would be foolish to turn back without investigating the moaning," Jupiter said decisively. He always hated to give up once he was on a trail.

"Come on, Pete. I'm going into the cave. You hold the rope until I'm inside."

Jupiter vanished under the water. The sun was almost down now, and in the darkening twilight Pete waited with the rope in his hands. When he felt a double tug, he fixed his mouthpiece in place and swam into the narrow passage.

There was little surf and no current and Pete's waterproof flashlight, which was fastened to his gear, gave plenty of illumination. The water in the tunnel became quickly shallow as the floor angled upward, and soon Pete was standing in the large cavern beside his friend. The first thing he noticed as he took off his swim fins was the sound.

"*Aaaaaaahhhhhhhhhhh—ooooooooooooooo—oooooo—oo!*"

The cave was moaning!

Jupiter was grinning like a contented cat. They were inside and the cave was actually moaning.

"Gosh, Jupe," Pete whispered, "you were right! No one saw us come inside, so the cave's moaning."

"It certainly seems that way, doesn't it?" Jupiter said somewhat smugly. "And it's just about twilight —the exact time of our first visit here last night. Come on!"

Quickly they took off their diving gear. Jupiter struck a match from his waterproof box and lighted two of the candles.

"We'll carry the candles to the mouths of all the tunnels that lead out of this cavern," Jupiter explained. "If the candle flickers, it means there is a current of air moving through the tunnel. If the flame doesn't move, that means the passage is probably blocked. It will save us a great deal of time and wasted searching."

Pete nodded. "Smart idea!"

Quickly they began to test the passages. At one, the candle flickered slightly. But Jupe was not satisfied. Pete went to the next tunnel. Suddenly the flame of his candle was drawn strongly into the dark opening.

"Here, Jupe!" Pete called excitedly.

"Shhhhhh!" whispered Jupiter. "We don't know

how close we may be to somebody."

Both boys held their breath and listened. For a long half-minute all was silent and Pete was furious at himself for shouting. Then the moan came again, faint but clear.

"*Aaaaaahhhhhhh—oooooooooooooo—ooooo—oo!*"

It seemed to come straight out of the tunnel that was attracting the candle flame. Jupiter took out his chalk and marked a small white question mark at the entrance to the passage. Then the two boys lit their flashlights and plunged into the tunnel.

Back at the cliff top, Bob sat with the dummies, watching the flaming orange sun set in the west. Slowly, a purple and red twilight settled over the ocean. Bob stretched his legs cautiously.

He had been sitting there talking to himself for over a half-hour, he guessed, and during all that time he had had the feeling that eyes were watching him. He knew that it was probably just his imagination, but it was a weird feeling anyway.

To occupy his mind, Bob began to read the book about Moaning Valley. He read the part that told of the mine shafts being sealed, and then he read farther. Suddenly he sat up very straight.

"Gosh!" he exclaimed in a whisper.

He had come to a passage about Old Ben Jackson and his partner, Waldo Turner. The book said that Old Ben and his partner lived on a ridge right next to Devil Mountain and that they had dug one of the mine shafts into the mountain. Their shaft had been sealed up with the others, but Old Ben and Waldo had refused to leave. They insisted they would keep prospecting for gold—and diamonds!

Bob frowned. He was sure that Jupiter, in his eagerness to get started on his plan, had not read this far in the book. If Jupe had read that Old Ben thought there were diamonds around Devil Mountain, he would have mentioned it.

In the growing darkness Bob was suddenly worried. Jupiter thought that the moaning might be caused by the reopening of one of the old shafts. Old Ben and his partner had actually dug such a shaft themselves, and they probably knew El Diablo's Cave better than anyone else, after living right next to it for so many years. It would be simple for them to reopen a shaft.

Then Bob thought about something else. He remembered how Old Ben had surprised them the previous night. They had been inside an *inner* cavern, yet Old Ben had claimed he was passing by *outside* the cave and heard them! Suddenly, Bob realized that this would have been practically impossible. The distance was too great. Old Ben must have been inside the cave when he heard them, which meant that he had lied to them.

Alarmed now, Bob dropped below the trail and hurriedly made a third dummy from the shirt, pants and sombrero that had originally been intended to represent him. Carefully, he pushed it into place beside the other two. In the dim twilight the three dummies should convince any observer that the boys were still seated there.

Then he crept through the underbrush until he felt it was safe to stand up and walk. He kept a good distance from the road, for he did not want to be seen. He felt it was very important that he get back to tell the Daltons what Pete and Jupe were doing in the cave. If Old Ben had actually found a diamond mine, they could be in real danger!

Bob hurried through the night as fast as he could with his injured leg and the difficult terrain. Before he had gone more than a few hundred yards he heard a soft sound in the night. It was a car driving slowly along the dirt road—without lights! It stopped no more than fifty feet from where Bob crouched.

A shadowy figure got out and walked rapidly toward Devil Mountain. The dark shape was dressed completely in black, and was all but invisible in the night. It quickly vanished.

Bob crept up to the parked car. It had a Nevada license plate.

Deep inside Devil Mountain, Pete and Jupe continued to track the moaning sound. After the first tunnel, they had come to another cavern and had again used their candles to locate the passage out. In the third cavern, smaller than any of the others, they had found three passages with air blowing through them. They decided not to split up. Instead, they searched each passage together.

The first tunnel ran straight ahead for quite a distance, then made a sudden, sharp turn.

"It's heading back toward the ocean, Jupe," Pete observed.

Jupiter frowned. "I don't think we want to go that way. I'm sure the moaning sound comes from closer to the valley side." He checked his compass. "We should go east or northeast, I think."

"This tunnel is heading southwest."

The boys retraced their steps and tried the second passage. Soon it, too, curved away toward the southwest. Once again they went back to the cavern. Pete was becoming impatient.

"Golly, Jupe, we could walk around in here forever!"

"Yes, but I'm sure we're on the right track. The moaning gets louder every time we move east."

Reluctantly Pete followed him into the third passage. The air current was strong and the moaning much louder. The tunnel went straight east! Jupiter pushed ahead as fast as was safe with only their flashlights. Suddenly both boys stopped in their tracks.

There was a gaping hole in the left wall, where a side passage joined the tunnel they were in.

"Gosh," Pete said, "that's the first side tunnel we've seen."

"Yes," Jupiter replied, examining it with his

flashlight, "and it's man-made—an old mine shaft that wasn't sealed at this end. Pete, look!"

The flame of Jupiter's candle was blowing strongly outward.

"What does that mean, Jupe?"

"It means," Jupiter whispered excitedly, "that somewhere down there is a third opening to the outside! Probably one of the old mine entrances has been secretly opened."

"Then why didn't the sheriff find it? Or Mr. Dalton?"

"I'm not sure, Pete," Jupiter admitted, "but——" His eyes suddenly widened as he listened to something.

Then Pete heard it, too—a faint sound of digging.

"Come on," Jupiter whispered, and started into the new passage.

As Pete prepared to follow, he suddenly became aware of the sound of footsteps behind him.

"Jupe," he quavered weakly.

Standing there, close behind them, was a small, thin man with burning dark eyes and a proud face— the face of little more than a boy. He wore a black sombrero, a short black jacket, a high-necked black shirt, and tight black trousers that flared at the bottom above shiny black boots.

He was the young man in the picture Professor Walsh had shown them at the ranch. El Diablo!

And he held a pistol in his left hand.

12.
Caught!

"Yipes!" cried Pete.

El Diablo pointed his pistol at Pete and made a sharp cutting motion in the air with his other hand.

"He wants us to be silent," Jupiter said, a little shakily.

El Diablo nodded. His boyish face showed no expression at all. He motioned with the pistol that he wanted the boys to walk ahead of him in the direction from which they had come, away from the sound of digging.

Reluctantly the two boys obeyed. They retraced their steps through the dark tunnel until they came to a cavern, where El Diablo motioned them to the right.

They walked and walked, along passages and through caverns. Although Pete knew by his watch that they had traveled for less than five minutes, it seemed more like five hours as he plodded along behind Jupiter. El Diablo, with his pistol, stayed just behind them.

"Halt!"

The command came sharply just as Pete and Jupiter entered another cavern. It was the first word El Diablo had spoken and it had a muffled, hollow sound.

The boys stopped. This cavern was smaller than most they had been in, and it had a gloomy, dank atmosphere.

"There!" El Diablo commanded in his muffled voice.

The bandit gestured toward a very narrow opening in the cavern wall. Jupiter and Pete looked at each other grimly, but there was nothing they could do. They marched into the narrow tunnel, with El Diablo close behind. They had taken only about ten steps when they came to a mound of rocks that completely blocked the passage. A dead end! Pete and Jupiter turned in dismay.

El Diablo's face was as rigid as stone. With a motion of his pistol, he indicated that they were to stand along the left wall. Then he quickly bent over and rolled a large rock away from the mound.

"Come!" the muffled voice commanded.

The boys walked to the hole that had been opened in the end of the passage, and Pete peered in. He saw nothing but a black hole. Before he could shine his flashlight inside, a strong shove sent him sprawling into the dark opening.

Pete landed hard on a stone floor. Something struck him in the ribs, and then he heard the stone being rolled back. Pete lay in total darkness behind the wall of rock.

"Pete?" It was Jupiter's voice beside him.

"I'm here," Pete answered, "but I wish I wasn't."

"I'm afraid he's walled us in," Jupe whispered in the darkness.

"I'm just plain afraid," Pete said.

At the edge of Moaning Valley, Bob was hurrying toward The Crooked-Y Ranch. Behind him, as if to spur him on, the valley continued to moan.

"Aaaaaahhhhhhhh—ooooooooooooo—oooooo —oo!"

Bob knew this meant that Jupiter's plan had worked. Pete and Jupe must be inside El Diablo's Cave by this time, yet the moaning had not stopped. After reading the book, however, Bob was almost sorry that the plan had succeeded. If his hunch was right, if Old Ben and his partner had something to do with the moaning sound, then Pete and Jupe could be in trouble.

Then there was the man in the car with the Nevada license plate. Who was he? Bob had seen only a dark shape walking toward Devil Mountain. He had waited for a time near the car, but the man had not come back. Bob had finally decided that too much was happening for the boys to carry on alone.

He hurried on toward the ranch. Once Moaning Valley was behind him, Bob decided to risk walking on the road, where he could make better time. Gradually the moaning faded in the distance. Then he heard a new sound behind him. A car was coming fast along the narrow dirt road. Just in time, Bob jumped for the cover of the bushes at the side of the road.

As the car roared past, he could not make out the face of the man bent close over the steering wheel, but he saw a black sombrero on his head. He also saw that it was the car with the Nevada license plate!

Alarmed, Bob hurried back onto the road. The Nevada car had been in a hurry. What had happened inside Devil Mountain? With a sinking feeling, Bob began to trot as fast as his injured leg would let him. He had to get to the ranch house right away. Maybe even Jupiter had gone too far this time.

"Uh—ooof!"

Bob had bumped headlong into a man who appeared suddenly in the road. Strong hands gripped his shoulders. He looked up into the long, scarred face of the man with the black eye patch.

Jupiter and Pete crouched in the darkness behind the wall of rock. From time to time they could still hear the moaning of the cave, distant and faint.

"Can you see anything?" Pete whispered.

"Not a thing. We're totally walled in, and——

Hey, are we crazy or something?" Suddenly Jupiter started to laugh.

"Gosh, Jupe, what's so funny?" Pete whispered.

"We're whispering," Jupiter said, "and sitting in the dark, but there's no one to hear us and we have our flashlights!"

The boys switched on their flashlights and grinned a little sheepishly at each other. Then Pete shone his light on the wall of rock.

"Maybe no one can hear us, and we have our lights, but how do we get out?" Pete asked.

Jupiter, as usual, refused to be discouraged. "First we'll see if we can push that big rock out. El Diablo did not appear to be exceptionally strong, yet he moved the stone with ease."

Pete tried to move the stone first. It would not budge. Then Jupiter joined him, and together the two boys applied all their strength. The boulder still did not move an inch. Panting, they finally gave up.

"He must have it wedged from the outside," Jupiter observed. "The more we push, the tighter we wedge it. He's locked us in tight."

"Great," Pete said. "What do you think, Jupe? Could he really be El Diablo? You know, the professor said he might still be alive."

"El Diablo may still be alive," Jupiter said, "but he wouldn't look like that. Remember, El Diablo would be almost a hundred years old. The man who caught us looked like El Diablo back in the 1880s!"

"Yes, I thought about that."

"In addition," Jupiter continued, "did you notice how his face never seemed to move? How he never showed any expression?"

"Sure I did, but——"

"I'm convinced that our captor was wearing a mask, Pete!" Jupiter said triumphantly. "One of those flesh-colored rubber masks that fit over the whole face. In addition, he spoke very little. I think he was afraid we might recognize his voice."

"I didn't. Did you, Jupe?"

"No," Jupiter admitted. "But I'm sure of one thing, anyway. He didn't want to harm us seriously, or he wouldn't have just imprisoned us in here."

"*Just* imprisoned us!" Pete objected. "Isn't that bad enough?"

"He could have done a lot worse," Jupiter pointed out a little grimly. "In here we'll be found sooner or later after we're missed, and he knows that. There's plenty of air. All he wanted was to have us out of the way for a short time, probably just tonight. Which means that we have to hurry and find our way out of here."

"Do you think it's safe yet, Jupe? Why don't we just let someone find us?" Pete asked.

"I'm convinced that the mystery has to be solved tonight," Jupiter insisted. "If we wait, it will be too late. Since we can't get out the way we came in, we have to see if going in the other direction leads us to some exit. Come on."

Pete followed Jupiter down the narrow passage. The tunnel continued straight ahead without any cross passages for what seemed like miles. Then suddenly the boys stopped and stared at each other in dismay. In front of them was another fall of rock. The passage was blocked at this end, too!

"Golly, Jupe!" Pete cried. "What do we try now?"

"I hadn't thought we would be blocked in so completely," the First Investigator said, and for the first time his round face looked worried. "It doesn't fit my deductions at all."

"Maybe El Diablo has different deductions," Pete observed.

Jupiter leaned down and carefully inspected the fall of rock. It, like all the others, was not recent. Jupiter bent closer. Suddenly he became excited.

"Pete, this big rock has been moved!"

Pete bent down and looked. From the marks on the floor there was no doubt that the big rock had been moved recently.

Together the boys strained at the boulder. It rocked slightly, but would not roll loose. Jupiter stood up and looked around.

"I think our friend used this passage to enter and leave the cave unseen. If the two of us can't move it, then there has to be some other way. . . . There! That long steel bar near the wall!"

Pete understood at once. A lever! He grabbed

the long bar and inserted it between the stone and the wall. Together the two boys leaned their weight on it and the great stone rolled away.

A gaping hole opened in front of them. Jupiter shone his light into the darkness.

"It's another cavern," he reported.

Pete dropped the long bar and both boys scrambled through the opening. They shone their flashlights around.

"Wow!" gasped Pete.

Jupiter just stared.

They were standing in an enormous cavern. In the center was a great black pool.

13.

The Pool of
The Old One

The pool glittered in the beams of their flashlights.

Pete swallowed hard. "The pool," he said in a low voice, "where The Old One lives."

"So there is a pool," Jupiter said. "It must have been blocked off a long time ago, but the Indians knew it was in the cave somewhere."

"And now we know, too, but I wish we didn't," Pete quavered. "Let's find a way out of here quick!"

"Just because the pool is really here doesn't mean that The Old One actually exists."

"It doesn't mean The Old One *doesn't* exist, either," Pete pointed out. "Maybe The Old One's been blocked off a long time, too. Maybe he's mad and hungry and just waiting for two smart boys."

Jupiter glanced around the dark cavern.

Shadows in the wall indicated more passages leading from the cavern.

"We'd better try to find a way out," Jupiter decided. "Light your candle and we'll test the openings."

"Now that's what I like to hear," Pete said.

He lit his candle and followed Jupiter. They tested two of the passages without success. Pete started to move on, but Jupiter stood still.

"Pete," he whispered.

Pete followed Jupiter's gaze. At first he could see nothing.

"There, against the wall," Jupiter hissed. It's ... it's ..."

Then Pete saw it—or rather, him! In a dark recess just inside the second passage, seated against the wall with his legs straight out in front of him was a small man, dressed all in black, with a sombrero on his head, and black boots on his feet. In his right hand the man held an ancient pistol, and his face was grinning straight at the boys.

Except that the face looking at them was not a face at all—it was a skull! And the hand that held the pistol was not a hand, it was five bones—a skeleton!

"Yow!" Pete cried. Both boys turned and ran. They reached the tunnel which had led them into the cavern and tried to scramble through the opening together. Both of them went down in a heap. "Where are we running to, Jupe?" mumbled Pete, on the bottom. "We can't get out this way!"

"Of course," replied Jupiter. "We weren't thinking clearly."

"I wasn't thinking, period," Pete said in a muffled voice. "Maybe you better get off me for a start."

"I would, but you're holding my leg," Jupiter said.

The boys untangled themselves, and sat up on the cold floor of the cavern. They were still shaking, but Pete began to grin.

"Boy, we're a couple of brave investigators!"

Jupiter nodded solemnly. "We panicked. A natural enough reaction under the circumstances, I believe. The accumulation of dangers resulted in a degree of nervousness that made us lose our rational responses. A skeleton is probably the least dangerous menace we have faced. We were simply at the point of panic."

Pete groaned. "It's too bad Bob isn't here to tell me what you just said."

"If he was here he'd tell you I said we were so tense from what's happened that we blew our tops," Jupiter said.

"You could have said that the first time."

"I could have, but it isn't exactly the meaning I wanted to communicate. However, that isn't what we should be concerned about now. I want to inspect that skeleton."

"I was afraid you'd want to do that." Pete followed Jupiter rather unwillingly over to where the skeleton seemed to grin at them from beneath the black sombrero. Warily, Jupe reached out and touched the sombrero. It crumbled into dry pieces.

"Golly!" Pete exclaimed, and touched the black jacket.

The jacket, too, crumbled and fell away from the skeleton. As Pete pulled his hand back, he brushed the bony fingers that held the gun. The fingers snapped off, and the pistol dropped to the floor with a loud, echoing clatter. Pete jumped back, but Jupiter bent closer to the skeleton.

"It's very old, Pete," Jupiter observed. "And that pistol is ancient too. . . . I would say that there is very little doubt about it."

"Very little doubt about what?"

"That this skeleton is El Diablo—the real El Diablo!" Jupiter's words echoed from the high ceiling of the cavern like some ghostly voice from the past.

"The real El Diablo?" Pete said. "You mean he was in here all the time but no one ever found him?"

Jupiter nodded. "I wouldn't be surprised if he died the very night he came into the cave. His wound must have been worse than anyone realized. Of course, in those days men often died from wounds we would consider minor today. Medical science has made great progress."

"But what makes you think he died that night?"

Pete asked, puzzled. "I mean, maybe he hid in here for years before he died."

Jupiter shook his head. "No, I don't believe so. First, you will notice that there are no signs of any food around the skeleton. He could have drunk water from the pool, although I would guess that the pool is salt water. Anyway, even if he had water there should be some evidence of food: bones, dried seeds, something."

"Maybe he ate and drank somewhere else," Pete suggested.

"Perhaps, but then what killed him? If he was in good health and was attacked there should be signs of a fight, and perhaps another skeleton or two. Also, if anyone had found El Diablo in the cave and killed him, surely the historical record would show that."

"Gee, I guess you're right," Pete agreed.

"In addition," Jupiter went on, "note the position of the skeleton. He literally died with his back to the wall. He was seated here ready to fight if any enemy appeared, but I don't think an enemy ever came. Look at the pistol."

Pete picked up the pistol. "It's full, Jupe. No shots fired."

"Just as I thought," Jupiter said in triumph. "His place of hiding was never discovered and he died alone in here of his wounds, just as the historical record states. Everything is consistent with that conclusion. El Diablo did know the cave better than anyone else."

"Maybe it would have been better for him if he hadn't known it so well," said Pete. "I mean, maybe if they'd found him they could have taken care of his wound."

"Perhaps, but you'll recall he was under sentence to hang anyway. I imagine he preferred dying in his cave to being recaptured. He may even have guessed that if he was never found his legend would grow, and perhaps in some way help his people."

"It sure grew," said Pete.

Jupiter nodded. "So much so that someone is now using it to scare us—and anyone else who comes into the cave. The question is why?"

"Maybe someone wants to make Mr. and Mrs. Dalton lose their ranch," Pete suggested.

"That's possible," Jupiter conceded, "but I don't think so. I think someone is trying to scare people away from the cave. Remember that the Daltons have been here for some time, but the moaning only started a month ago."

"Golly, Jupe, if someone is trying to scare people away, how come no one saw the phony El Diablo until tonight? I mean, why didn't he appear when the sheriff and Mr. Dalton explored the cave?"

"I don't know that yet," Jupiter admitted. "But until tonight the moaning always stopped when anyone entered the cave. Tonight we managed to enter unseen, the moaning did not stop, and the fake El Diablo appeared! This leads me to the deduction that we saw El Diablo tonight *because* the moaning had not stopped."

"That makes less sense than anything else." Pete protested. "What do you think it means?"

For once Jupiter looked completely baffled. "I don't know, Pete. But I do know that there is more to the mystery of Moaning Valley than some natural cause for the moaning. We have to find out what that digging we heard earlier was all about."

"Gosh, I'd forgotten all about the digging. Do you really think there's a diamond mine in the cave?"

"I think someone is trying to conceal something," Jupiter explained. "Last night I found a diamond. Tonight we heard somebody digging. Logic indicates that a diamond mine must be involved somehow."

"Maybe we should tell Mr. Dalton what we know, Jupe," Pete said uneasily.

Jupiter frowned. The First Investigator hated to admit that they could not handle a situation on their own, but even he had to agree that there were times when three boys could not do the job alone.

"I suppose you're right," Jupiter said reluctantly. "Bring El Diablo's pistol and we'll try to find the tunnel that leads out of here."

Pete lit his candle, and the boys started for the next tunnel to test for a current of air.

Suddenly there was a faint ripple in the water of the pool that had been so dark and silent. This was followed by splashing and loud breathing. The boys stood motionless, their flashlights trained on the sound.

A black and shiny shape broke the surface of the murky pool. Water dripped from its shining skin, reflecting in the beams of the boys' flashlights, as the creature raised itself out of the water.

Jupiter and Pete stared in horror as the shiny black creature began to climb out of the pool.

14.

The Black and Shiny Creature

"What are you boys doing here?" the creature demanded.

Suddenly, at the same time, both boys realized what they were looking at. It was a man wearing a black rubber wet-suit, swim fins, a double air tank painted black, and a black rubber mask that completely covered his face.

"Oh, boy!" Pete exploded in relief.

Jupiter, recovering immediately, drew himself up to his full height, his round face suddenly looking much older. It was an old trick he used when dealing with adults, and it usually worked as well as his other surprises.

"What, sir, are *you* doing here?" he asked in his deepest voice. "We are here by permission of the owners of this ranch. You, apparently, have come in

113

by some secret entrance that leads from the sea. You are trespassing."

The skin diver reached up and removed his rubber face mask. He was a handsome, blond man and he was grinning at Jupiter. Unhooking his air tanks, he laid them on the floor.

"Well, son, you sound almost as important as the admiral," he said. "I wasn't questioning your right to be here. I was just wondering what two boys were doing in El Diablo's Cave this late at night."

"The admiral?" Jupiter looked puzzled for a moment. "Of course! You're a frogman aren't you? A Navy frogman on training maneuvers with those ships out near the islands."

The frogman looked serious. "Yes, that's exactly what I am. We're on a highly secret training mission here. I'll have to swear you boys to complete secrecy. Have you seen anything in the water you thought was unusual?"

"No," Pete said.

"Nothing, sir," Jupiter assured him. Then, remembering suddenly, he snapped his fingers. "Except that shape!"

"Shape?" the frogman repeated.

Now Pete remembered, too. "That long, black thing that passed us out in the ocean."

"It was a submarine, Pete!" Jupiter exclaimed eagerly. "A midget submarine. That was why it was so rigid, and why it moved so steadily. But why didn't we hear its engines? Sound carries very far under water."

The frogman's face darkened. "This could be very serious, boys. That submarine you saw is top secret—especially the silence of its engines. I'm afraid I'll have to hold you."

"Hold us?" Pete echoed.

"A submarine that moves so silently that it can't be detected by sonar is very important Pete," Jupiter said solemnly. "However, I believe we can prove that there is no need to hold us, Mr. . . ."

"Commander Crane," the frogman said. "Commander Paul Crane. And I'm sorry, but I am going to have to hold you—at least until the admiral can have you investigated."

Jupiter nodded understandingly and tried to look dignified, which wasn't easy when he was wearing only bathing trunks and a diving belt.

"We're Jupiter Jones and Pete Crenshaw," Jupiter said, and reached into one of the waterproof containers which hung from his diving belt. "I believe these credentials will attest to our complete reliability."

Jupiter handed the commander the boys' business card and the special deputy cards given to them by Chief Reynolds of the Rocky Beach police. Commander Crane studied the cards.

"We happen to be involved in an important case right now," Jupiter told him. "That is why we are in this cave. I'm sure your admiral would want you to cooperate with us, Commander."

Commander Crane looked at Jupiter and hesitated. The First Investigator could be very impressive when he was being serious and professional.

"Well now," the frogman said, "these cards do make you boys seem legitimate."

"Why don't you communicate with your ship," Jupiter suggested "and have them check at once with Chief Reynolds in Rocky Beach. I'm sure he will vouch for us."

"Gosh, Jupe," Pete exclaimed, "how can the commander talk to his ship from in here?"

"A good frogman is always in contact with his ship," Jupiter informed Pete. "I assume that the commander has some form of long-range radio."

Commander Crane smiled. "You're a very smart boy, I see. All right, you boys just sit down and stay put."

Jupiter and Pete did as they were told, and Commander Crane vanished into the darkness. Minutes passed. The boys could barely see the frogman crouched in the dark of the cavern. He was bending over a tiny instrument of a type the boys had never seen before. Jupiter watched with curiosity, but he could not make out what was happening.

As last the commander straightened up again, replaced his instrument in a hidden pocket, and strode back to the boys. He was smiling.

"Security says you boys check out," he said. "I won't have to hold you."

"Gosh, you move fast," Pete said.

"We move fast when we have to," replied Commander Crane. "The admiral has pretty high priorities."

"Now that we've been approved, Commander," Jupiter said seriously, "may we ask you some questions?"

"Me?" The frogman shook his head, smiling. "I'm afraid that won't be possible, boys. My work is also highly secret."

"It's not about your work exactly, sir," Jupiter assured him. "I want to know about this cave. First, was it you Pete saw last night up near the front of the cave?"

Commander Crane nodded. "It was probably one of my men. He reported that he had been briefly spotted."

"That makes me feel better," Pete said. "At least it explains another mystery of the cave."

"Second," Jupiter went on, "did you or your men make any changes inside the cave? I mean, did you change the layout of the cave, the various tunnels and openings, or anything like that?"

"No," the commander said, "I can tell you that much."

"Third, sir," Jupiter enumerated, "is anything you are doing causing the cave to moan as it does?"

"Absolutely not. We wondered about that moaning ourselves. Of course, we've only been in the cave a few times. We haven't been in this area long. We assumed the cave always moaned like that."

"And your work requires you to remain completely unseen if possible?" Jupiter pressed on.

"Absolutely." The commander smiled. "As a matter of fact, I'm sure we haven't been seen by anyone but you boys. Most of our work has been done on the ocean side of the cave, and here near this pool."

"Have you seen anyone else in the cave?" Jupiter asked.

Commander Crane shook his head. "No, it is essential to our training mission that we remain unseen. Of course, there is no enemy here, but we try to avoid any contact with anyone."

"Of course," Jupiter said with a sound of disappointment.

"I'm sorry, boys," Commander Crane said. "I'd like to have helped you. Can you find your way out of this cavern?"

"We've been trying to find our way," Pete blurted out. "That's what we were doing when we saw you."

"Well, I think I can set you on the right track," the commander said. "Remember, you must not talk about anything you have seen here involving our operation."

"Yes, sir!" Pete agreed.

"Of course, Commander," echoed Jupiter.

"All right, then, follow me." The frogman led the boys to one of the tunnel openings, then through several caverns and side passages until they emerged into the large cavern where Pete had first seen the mysterious black and shiny shape.

"All right, boys," Commander Crane said. "I expect you can make it from here. I must get back to my work."

"Thank you, sir," said Jupiter.

The frogman smiled at them. "And good luck with *your* work."

He vanished back into the small opening, and Pete started for the tunnel that he remembered led out to Moaning Valley.

Jupiter made no move to follow. He was staring into empty space with that faraway look Pete knew only too well.

"Oh no!" Pete groaned. "Don't tell me, Jupe."

"I'm more certain than ever that we have to solve the mystery tonight, Pete," Jupiter said. "The man disguised as El Diablo knew we would find our way out eventually. That means he didn't care how much we knew as long as we couldn't get in his way until some hours from now."

"I don't want to get in his way at all," Pete observed, "but something tells me I'm going to."

"This is our real opportunity Pete," Jupiter insisted. "Whoever is trying to scare people off thinks we're still out of the way! We'll never have a better chance to locate that digging and find out what makes the cave moan."

"I guess you're right," Pete said dubiously. "Only maybe we'd better go and get Mr. Dalton and the other men first."

"If we leave the cave we'll be seen," Jupiter pointed out. "Besides, there isn't time. We've got to move fast now with the advantage we have."

"Some advantage," Pete said, "but I guess you're right, Jupe. Where do we start? I mean, we've been here before, and we didn't know which way to go."

"But this time we have more information," Jupiter said confidently. "This time we know that the digging has something to do with the moaning."

"How do you figure that?" Pete asked, mystified.

"Because neither the sheriff nor the Daltons nor the newspaper mentioned a word about any digging. So whoever is digging is doing it in secret. By deduction, it has to be connected with the moaning sound because it is the only activity that goes on secretly in the cave when no one is here!"

"Well . . ." Pete remained unconvinced.

"Two unexplained facts in the same place almost certainly must be connected," Jupiter persisted.

Pete's eyes widened. "Sure, okay. What do we do then?"

"First, you can use your keen sense of direction to find that side passage where we heard the digging."

Pete nodded. Mentally he retraced their steps since they had been captured by El Diablo. At last he said, "Jupe, I figure we have to find a passage that will take us northwest."

"That way," said Jupiter, looking at his compass and pointing to the left.

"Right," Pete confirmed. "Let's go!"

The two boys lit their candles, forgetting their earlier caution in the excitement of being so near to a solution of the mystery. As they approached the opening in the northwest wall, a sound came out as if to greet them.

"*Aaaaaahhhhhhhhh—oooooooooooo—oooooo —ooo!*"

"The moaning!" Pete whispered.

"It never stopped, Pete. We've just become accustomed to it."

"It sure seems closer now."

"Because it's coming from that tunnel!" Jupiter held his candle in the tunnel entrance. A strong draft of air blew the flame, and with it the moan came again.

"*Aaaaaahhhhhhhhh—oooooooooooo—oooooo —ooo!*"

The two boys plunged into the passage, which soon led into a small cavern.

"I know where we are now, Jupe," Pete said in a low tone.

"Blow out your candle, then," whispered Jupiter. "We'll use our flashlights."

The boys covered their flashlights with their hands so that only a faint glow could be seen, and Pete led the way into the same tunnel through which the fake El Diablo had taken them earlier. The moan grew louder as they walked.

"*Aaaaaahhhhhhhhh—oooooooooooo—oooooo —ooo!*"

As they approached the cross passage, they heard the sound of digging.

"Golly." Pete gulped. "We really did hear digging."

"Of course we did. Come on!" whispered Jupiter.

They plunged ahead into the man-made tunnel, moving as silently as possible. It was long and straight. At the end of it they saw a glow of light. Jupiter motioned for Pete to slow down.

The glow of light came from a hole in the side wall of the mineshaft. Rocks and boulders lay in piles all around it. The sound of digging was coming from the hole.

Cautiously the boys crept forward and peered into the hole, blinking at the bright light.

At that moment the moaning came again—so loud that the sound was painful to their ears. It echoed all around them, then gradually died away.

"Gosh!" Pete whispered. "It hurt my ears."

Jupiter caught Pete's arm. "Look!"

Their eyes had adjusted to the bright light inside

the cavern, and they could see a figure bending over with a shovel in his hand.

Pete gulped.

The figure suddenly straightened, put down his shovel, and picked up a pickaxe. For a moment he was clearly visible in the light of his electric lantern —a man with white hair and a flowing white beard.

Old Ben Jackson.

15.

Part of the Mystery Solved

Through the opening in the side wall, Pete and Jupiter watched Old Ben working inside the secret cavern. Every few minutes, at irregular intervals, the moaning shattered their ears. The noise did not seem to bother the old man at all. He kept digging at the base of the cavern wall with his pickaxe.

"Look," Jupiter whispered. "It looks like another rock fall."

"It's a big one," Pete whispered back.

"You see how those breaks in the rocks are sharp and clean?" Jupiter pointed out. "That fall happened very recently."

Old Ben continued his work at the fall, unaware of the eyes watching him. The old prospector swung his axe with vigor and surprising strength for a man of his age. Then he put it down again, and picked up the shovel.

"Jupe!" hissed Pete. "Look at his eyes."

The eyes of the old prospector gleamed wildly in the light of his electric lantern, just as they had the previous night when the old man had warned them against The Old One.

"Gold fever," Jupiter said softly, "or, in this case, diamond fever. I've read that prospectors often get like that when they think they have a strike. Nothing can get in their way or stop them."

"Gosh," Pete whispered.

Old Ben turned again to the wall and dug steadily at the fallen rock loosened by his pickaxe. He shoveled it into a kind of tilted sieve. Every few minutes, while the boys watched, he bent down and picked something out of the dirt. Each time, he examined the object, laughed wildly, and put it into a small leather bag near the electric lantern.

"Are they diamonds?" Pete whispered.

"I expect so," Jupiter responded in the same low voice. Old Ben was so involved in his work that he probably wouldn't have heard the boys if they had spoken normally, but they were taking no chances.

"Then he *has* found a diamond mine," Pete said.

Jupiter was staring at the rock fall, his round face furrowed with thought.

"It looks that way, Pete, only——"

"What else could it be? He's struck a diamond mine, and he knows it's on Crooked-Y property. If anyone found out about it he'd at least have to share the diamonds with the Daltons, wouldn't he? Maybe legally they all belong to Mr. and Mrs. Dalton. So he only digs at night, and he scares everyone away from the cave!"

Jupe nodded slowly. "I guess you're right, Pete. That explains everything except——"

"Except why the cave moans," Pete interrupted. "And what makes it stop when anyone comes inside."

"I wasn't thinking of that," Jupiter said, "but I think I can explain why the moaning stops. You see, the sheriff and Mr. Dalton must have found this mine shaft all right. Only they didn't find the place where Old Ben is working."

As Pete opened his mouth to ask a question, a bell began to ring insistently in the hollow cave.

Old Ben dropped his shovel and moved with amazing speed to a small box near his lantern. He touched something on the box and the clanging bell stopped. Then he picked up his lantern and the small leather bag and headed straight for the hole in the wall where Pete and Jupiter were crouching.

"Quick, Pete!" Jupiter whispered urgently.

The two boys scrambled back to hiding places behind the loose mounds of rock in the shaft. They were none too fast. They had barely gotten out of sight when Old Ben came through the hole in the wall. The old man laid down his lantern and leather bag, and picked up a long steel bar the boys had not noticed on the floor of the shaft.

At that moment the moan began once more.

"*Aaaaahhhhhhhhh—oooo———*"

But this time the spooky sound stopped before it was finished. Old Ben had rolled a large boulder into the opening, using the bar as a lever. With the rock in place there was no trace of the opening. And the moaning stopped abruptly!

"Gosh, Jupe," Pete said. "That's what you meant! No one could tell there was a hole in that wall."

The large boulder fit tightly into the gap as if it had always been there.

"Right," Jupiter whispered, "and the blocking of the hole stops the moaning right away. That bell must be the signal from whoever is watching up on the mountain. I think it means someone is coming into the cave."

"Maybe Bob got scared and went for help," Pete said. "I hope."

Old Ben was pacing up and down in the mine shaft, muttering to himself. He didn't even glance toward the rocks where the boys were hiding. Then, suddenly, the old man switched off his lantern. For a moment there was no sound in the dark mine shaft; then the boys heard the pacing and muttering begin again. They waited tensely in their hiding place.

In the darkness, Pete tried to sort out everything he had learned that evening. There were still questions he wanted to ask Jupiter, but Pete thought he understood most of the answers to the mystery of Moaning Valley.

Old Ben was digging secretly in the cave. Up on the mountain someone was on guard. The moaning sound was produced by the wind blowing through the narrow opening of the prospector's secret cavern. When someone came to the cave, the guard signaled with the bell and Old Ben closed up the hole. The moaning sound stopped and there was no clue to what caused the moaning.

Pete felt quite pleased with himself for figuring it all out. He had answered all the questions himself . . . or had he? Who, for instance, was the fake El Diablo who had captured them? And how did he fit into the puzzle? Was that what Jupe had been referring to when he said something was still unexplained?

"Pete!" Jupiter's voice whispered in his ear. "Someone is coming!"

Pete was so startled he almost lost his balance. He grabbed at the big rock in front of him, and a small stone rolled to the ground. Had Old Ben heard the noise? Pete held his breath.

A moment later he saw a bobbing light approaching.

"Waldo?" Old Ben's voice said from somewhere nearby.

"Yup," a voice replied from behind the bobbing light. "They's two of 'em coming in the cave, Ben. We best skedaddle."

Old Ben's lantern came on, and Jupiter and Pete could see the tall, thin figure of Waldo Turner. The boys crouched as low behind the rocks as they could get. The two old men stood less than ten feet from them now.

"You sure they're comin' in?" Old Ben asked.

"I'm sure. Too dang many people foolin' around this cave the last couple days," Waldo replied.

"Jumpin' bobcats!" Old Ben exclaimed. "And I figure not more'n a few more days' work 'fore we're finished. Well, no sense gettin' careless now. We better get on out."

"We better," Waldo agreed.

It was clear that Waldo Turner was the man on watch on top of Devil Mountain. After giving the alarm, he had come down by some secret passage from the top.

The boys watched the two old prospectors move the boulder away from the hole, pass quickly through, and lever the rock back into the hole from the inside. Then there was silence in the pitch-black mine shaft.

"Where did they go, Jupe?" Pete whispered.

"There must be an exit from that cavern to the outside of the mountain. There would have to be. The wind wouldn't be able to make that moaning sound if it couldn't blow through from the other side. It's probably one of those old mine shafts that are supposed to be sealed up. I'll bet Old Ben and Waldo knew just where those shafts were and unsealed one."

"How come the sheriff and Mr. Dalton don't

know it's there?" Pete asked.

"It's probably concealed," guessed Jupiter. "There has to be another entrance up high on the mountain, too, for Waldo to get down here so fast. There are probably quite a few hidden entrances. However, I think it's time we went for help."

"Let's go!" Pete agreed fervently.

The boys switched on their flashlights and walked rapidly back along the mine shaft. By retracing their steps, they soon reached the first large cavern they had entered the previous night.

As they hurried toward the tunnel that would lead them outside, two figures leaped out of the shadows. Strong hands closed on Pete's arm.

"Got you!" a harsh voice grunted.

Pete gulped in fright as his light shone up into the long, scarred face of the man with the eye patch.

"Run, Jupe!" Pete cried.

At the same instant, a flashlight was suddenly beamed on Jupiter by the second man.

"Don't move, son," the scar-faced man said.

16.
A Tale of Diamonds

"Just stay where you are," the man with the eye patch commanded. "If you start running around in the dark you'll get hurt."

Jupiter braved it out. "I doubt that you would care if I *were* hurt. I suggest you let us go. We have friends here."

The man laughed. "Spunky, aren't you? . . . Why don't you come over here where we can have a talk."

"Don't, Jupe!" Pete cried.

And then a familiar voice spoke from behind the flashlight of the second man.

"It's okay, fellows. Mr. Reston is a detective!"

The voice was Bob's and his face was one big

131

grin when he came out into the light and saw the astonished looks of his partners.

"I started for the ranch to get help after I saw that the man in the Nevada car was going into the cave," Bob explained. He went on to describe his sudden hunch that Old Ben and Waldo were involved in the mystery of Moaning Valley. "After the Nevada car passed me I was scared and ran right into Mr. Reston here."

"Sam Reston," the man with the eye patch introduced himself. "I'm a detective, boys, working for an insurance company. When your friend here told me of his suspicions about Old Ben, I decided to come back to the cave with him instead of going all the way to the ranch for help."

"Mr. Reston thought you might need help right away," Bob explained.

"I did," Reston said, "because the man I'm after is very dangerous. Bob and I tried to get into the cave unseen. It took us some time, and I think we were seen anyway."

"You were, Mr. Reston," Jupiter said, suddenly recovering his voice. The First Investigator told Bob and Mr. Reston about everything he and Pete had seen in the cave.

Reston nodded. "I was afraid we'd been spotted. But they can't have gone far, and that bag you saw probably contains the diamonds I'm after."

"What diamonds?" Pete burst out.

"That's the job I'm on, boys," Reston explained.

"I'm trying to find a very clever jewel thief who stole a fortune in diamonds. His name is Laslo Schmidt, and he is known all over Europe. I followed his trail here to Santa Carla just a week ago. Then I heard about Moaning Valley and El Diablo's Cave, and I had the idea that the cave would be a good place for Schmidt to hide. Only I haven't found a trace of him."

"Gosh," Pete said, "if you followed his trail here, why couldn't you spot him?"

"Because I have no idea what he looks like now," Reston told them. "You see, boys, about five years ago Schmidt left Europe in a hurry. The International Police, Interpol, learned that he had come to America and assumed a new identity. But that was all they could find out. Schmidt is a master of disguise and impersonation. He could act the part of almost anyone and make you believe it."

Jupiter had his faraway thoughtful expression. "And he stole some diamonds insured by your company, Mr. Reston?"

"Yes, about a year ago. He hadn't stolen anything since he left Europe, and the police thought that he had given up, or perhaps even died. But when the diamonds were stolen we knew at once that Schmidt was the thief. The way it was done, it could have been no one else."

"The *modus operandi,* or method of operation is very important," agreed Jupiter. "That is how most criminals are caught, especially professional thieves. A thief can never really change his way of committing a theft except in minor details."

"That's right, Jupiter," Reston acknowledged. "The theft was obviously the work of Laslo Schmidt, and we realized that he had been simply biding his time. It became clear that he had spent his years in this country establishing a new identity. So now he is actually two men: Schmidt the thief, and some other person who is perfectly normal and above suspicion."

"And you don't know what this other identity is," Bob put in quickly. "It could be anyone around here."

Reston nodded. "Exactly, Bob. I traced him through the sale of two of the diamonds. First to Reno, Nevada, and then here."

"Nevada!" Pete and Bob both exclaimed at once.

"Gosh," Pete added, "we thought *you* were driving that Nevada car that forced us over the cliff."

"No, boys," Reston explained. "I was on my way to Moaning Valley when I saw your bikes at the edge of the pass. I stopped to see what was wrong, and would have rescued you, but then I saw those other people coming and knew you'd be okay. At that time I didn't want to reveal my presence here. You see, I think Schmidt spotted me in Nevada. I tried to fool him by putting on this eye patch and pasting a false scar on my face before coming to

Santa Carla. I'm not sure my disguise was success-
ful, though."

"That's why you've been sort of hiding?" Bob
asked.

"That's right. I didn't want Schmidt to know I
was still on his trail."

While Reston had been talking, Jupiter had
been staring off into the dark spaces of the cavern
and biting his lip. Now an eager gleam came into
his eyes.

"The diamonds he stole," Jupiter said slowly.
"There is something special about them, isn't there,
Mr. Reston?"

Reston looked at him in astonishment. "Why,
yes, Jupiter, there is. You see, they weren't stolen
from any jewelry company or store. They were taken
from a special display at a museum in San Francisco.
They——"

"—— are *rough* diamonds!" Jupiter completed
the sentence for him. "They are uncut, exactly as
they came from the diamond mine, correct? They
are also industrial diamonds."

"I don't understand how you know," Reston
said, "but you're right about their being rough diamonds. Only a few are just industrial stones, though.
You see, the display was made up of diamonds from
all over the world, just as they came out of the
ground. Because they look like ordinary rocks, and
because they were in a museum, they were not very

well guarded. Schmidt had no trouble stealing them. Most of them are gemstones, very valuable and just about unidentifiable since they are rough. But how did you know, Jupiter?"

"Because I found a rough diamond here in the cave," Jupiter said, "and because I think Old Ben and Waldo have found the rest of them!"

"Then the stones really are in the cave!" Reston exclaimed.

Jupiter nodded solemnly. "I think your Laslo Schmidt hid them here right after he stole them. He probably planned to keep them hidden until everyone gave up the chase. Only Old Ben and Waldo, prospecting secretly in the cave as they have probably been doing for years, found them and thought that they had uncovered a diamond mine!"

"But there are no diamond mines in this area," Reston pointed out.

"No, sir, but Old Ben and Waldo have always believed that there are diamonds here. I remember Mr. Dalton said they have been looking for precious stones as well as gold and silver. The diamonds Schmidt stole look exactly as they would if they had just been dug up, don't they?"

"Yes, they do," Reston admitted, "but wouldn't Ben and Waldo have suspected something odd when they found all the diamonds hidden in one place?"

Jupiter nodded eagerly. "Yes, but I don't think Old Ben found them that way! We are right on top of the San Andreas Fault here, as you know. The cave is filled with the debris of large earthquakes that occurred some years ago. We haven't had a large quake for many years, but small ones are always happening."

"You mean you think there was an earthquake here just recently?" Pete asked.

"Yes, I do. I think that a small earthquake about a month ago disturbed the hiding place of the diamonds. Old Ben and Waldo, digging as usual, found the diamonds scattered in the dirt and thought that they had found a mine!"

"Wow!" Pete exclaimed.

Reston nodded. "Yes, it's quite possible. However, boys, you must remember that a detective has to consider *all* possible explanations, and there is another possibility. Old Ben or Waldo may have stolen the diamonds themselves, and are now only recovering them after the earthquake buried them."

Jupiter reddened. "Of course, I should have considered that."

"But, Mr. Reston," Bob said, "Old Ben and Waldo have been here a long time! They're local characters. They couldn't have come from Europe only five years ago."

Reston smiled. "Remember, Bob, that I said Laslo Schmidt is a master of disguise and impersonation! He could be impersonating one of them."

"Gosh, of course," Bob agreed.

"However, I think there is only one way to find out," said Reston. "We'll go back to that cavern where Ben and Waldo were digging and see if we can find out where they went. But first, I think one of you boys had better go back to the ranch and call the sheriff. We're going to have evidence to show him."

Jupiter nodded. "I think Pete had better go."

Pete's face fell. "Just when we're going to finish the case!" he protested.

"Jupiter is right," Reston said. "Bob's leg isn't in good shape, and I want Jupiter with me. Besides, I can see that you're the fastest, Pete. On a team, each man has to do what he does best."

Still reluctant, but pleased with the tribute to his athletic prowess, Pete obeyed. He slipped quietly out of the cave, and began to run at a steady pace toward The Crooked-Y ranchhouse.

Inside the cave, Jupiter, Bob and Sam Reston walked quickly through the tunnels until they stood in front of Old Ben's secret cavern. Reston moved the boulder, and stepped into the cavern.

The little room was empty. But in the far wall, they found Old Ben and Waldo's exit tunnel. It was another man-made mine shaft, and it angled sharply upward. With Sam Reston in the lead, his pistol ready, they started through the tunnel. Jupiter marked another trail of chalk question marks.

"We're heading toward the north ridge of the mountain," Bob said as they advanced. "That's where the book says Old Ben and Waldo have their cabin."

"That is to be expected, Bob," Jupiter observed. "They opened an old mine shaft close to their cabin so there would be less chance of being observed."

Reston suddenly stopped. Ahead, the shaft ended in a wall of rocks. Bob noticed footprints on the ground that seemed to go straight into the wall of stones. Reston bent close. He leaned against a boulder and moved it out of the way. Then he moved two more large stones until there was a small passage.

The detective crawled into the passage. For a moment his feet were visible to the boys, and then they vanished. Bob and Jupiter peered into the hole, then quickly scrambled through.

They stood in the clear night behind a thick cover of trees and bushes on the north ridge of Devil Mountain.

"No one would notice a hole that small in the mountain," Reston observed. "Come on, boys, but stay behind me."

The detective advanced cautiously along the ridge between the valley and the sea. In a minute they saw a gleam of light in the window of a small cabin. They crept quietly up to the window and looked in. Old Ben and Waldo sat at a bare table, a pile of small stones between them!

17.
Jupiter Guesses Right

His pistol in his hand, Sam Reston opened the door of the cabin.

"Claim jumpers!" cried Old Ben in his high, cracked voice. "Get 'em, Waldo!"

Sam Reston leveled his pistol. "Just sit where you are, Waldo."

The tall old prospector was half out of his chair. He slowly sat down again.

"The maverick's got the drop on us, Ben," Waldo said.

"We gonna let him get away with claim robbing?" Old Ben demanded.

"No one fights fair no more, Ben," Waldo complained.

The two old men glared furiously at Reston.

Then Old Ben's wild red eyes fixed on Bob and Jupiter.

"Those boys!" he cried. "I told you they was fixin' to cause trouble, Waldo! We should have taken care of them!"

"I guess you were right," Waldo agreed.

Old Ben waved his arms wildly. "You mavericks can't get away with this, you hear? Always get claim jumpers, yessir. Hang 'em high, that's what we do!"

"The mine's ours," Waldo insisted, touching the small pile of rough diamonds on the table.

"Is that why you had to sneak into the cave?" Reston demanded. "Is that why you dug at night and closed that cavern every time anyone came?"

Old Ben's eyes grew cunning. "A rich strike, yessir. Got to keep it quiet. Word gets out, we got a stampede on our hands. No sir, we keep it quiet."

Bob said hotly, "You wanted it quiet because this land belongs to Mr. and Mrs. Dalton! The diamonds are theirs!"

"We been prospecting that cave almost twenty years." Waldo protested. "We found the diamonds. We dug 'em out. They belong to us, you hear me, boy?"

All this time Jupiter had said nothing. He was looking intently around the cabin. He was intrigued to see that it contained a radio, a bookcase full of books, and stacks of newspapers. He picked up one of the newspapers and studied it.

Old Ben's red-rimmed eyes grew even more shrewd.

"Tell you what, there's enough for everyone, right?" he said in his high voice. "Sure, plenty to go around. Now, we're not so greedy. Tell you what, we'll split with you, eh? A quarter of these stones here, and you can dig with us in the mine, eh? Lots more stones in there. A bonanza!"

Suddenly Jupiter spoke up. "There are no more stones, Mr. Jackson, or only a few, and you are quite aware of that."

Everyone turned to stare at Jupiter.

"This cabin is not entirely consistent with your pose as two eccentric old prospectors living in the past," Jupiter went on.

"Gosh, Jupe, what do you mean?" Bob exclaimed.

"He means these old codgers are partial fakes," Sam Reston said, "which I suspect is true. But how did you reach that conclusion, Jupiter?"

Jupiter pointed to the radio. "A portable radio scarcely fits in with the picture of two crazy old men with nothing on their minds but the past. And the books in this bookcase indicate an alertness and interest in the modern world they aren't supposed to have. I would say they have found the people in the area a soft touch, contributing to their grubstake without asking any questions. And I am also certain that they were aware that they had not found a diamond mine."

"How do you figure that, Jupiter?" Reston asked.

Jupe indicated the bookcase. "Four of the books in that bookcase are about diamonds, and all four are quite new. In addition, this newspaper contains a full account of the San Francisco diamond robbery from the museum! It is dated a year ago, and the story is circled in pencil. It's a San Francisco paper, so they must have obtained it specially."

"So!" Reston turned to the two old men. "What do you have to say to that?"

Old Ben and Waldo looked at each other. Finally Old Ben shrugged. When he spoke this time his voice did not sound at all eccentric.

"The boy's right," Old Ben said simply. "We knew it wasn't a diamond mine. No diamonds around here."

"We thought maybe it was a strike when we found the first couple," Waldo added, "only we really knew better, so Ben got those books. The diamonds turned out to be mostly African types. Then I went to the library and found a small piece in the local paper about that robbery. We got a copy of the San Francisco paper, and it described the stones, so we knew they were from the robbery."

Old Ben took up the story. "The diamonds were stolen, so we figured we could keep them. No one except the crook was going to know. We started to dig and found a real bonanza!"

"Only the holes we opened up made the cave

start to moan again," Waldo went on. "At first we figured that was fine, it scared folks away from the cave. Then Mr. Dalton and the sheriff started looking around. So I went up on the mountain and any time anyone came near the cave I signaled Ben and he closed up the holes until they went away."

Old Ben chuckled. "We sure had everyone fooled. I scared you boys off once myself, only I don't figure how you got into the cave tonight without Waldo seeing you."

Jupiter explained the ruse of Bob and the dummies, and the two old men listened with admiration. Old Ben chuckled when Jupe finished.

"By jinkers, I said you boys was smart, yessir. You had it figured, and you foxed us pretty good."

Reston spoke sternly. "This is not a laughing matter, Mr. Jackson. Keeping stolen property is a serious crime."

Ben grinned sheepishly. "I don't know if we'd really have kept them. Only we'd never made a real strike, and it was kind of exciting to dig them up. For a while we felt like real prospectors again. I guess it wasn't right, only we figured no one would be hurt except the thief. At least not until we decided what to do with the stones."

"What about those accidents?" Bob asked hotly. "And the rock that almost hit us?"

"Most of them were real accidents," Waldo explained. "They happen around here all the time.

People got nervous from the moaning and that made them more careless. The one that almost hit you was my fault, though. I was watching you and my foot knocked over a stone and the boulder fell. I never meant to hurt anyone."

Sam Reston looked at the two men severely. "I'll decide what to do about you two later," he said, gathering up the diamonds and putting them back into the leather bag. The two old men watched wistfully as their rich strike vanished.

"You've acted foolishly," added Reston, "but you did recover the diamonds. Maybe you meant to return them eventually, who knows? Just now I have a thief to find."

Jupiter spoke up again. "I've been thinking about Schmidt, Mr. Reston. I'm positive he knows Old Ben and Waldo have been digging in the cave, and he must know they have found his diamonds. I'm sure he will be back to get them, which leads me to think you can set a trap for him."

The muffled voice spoke from close behind them all.

"You are a smart boy. I did return!"

Everyone jumped, and turned toward the voice. There in the doorway stood the fake El Diablo! His masked face was as young and rigid as when he had captured Jupiter and Pete in the cave, and his left hand held the same pistol aimed at them all.

"Don't move, boys," Reston said quietly. "If this

is Schmidt, he is a dangerous man." The detective was eying his own pistol, which he had left on the table.

"Very wise advice," the muffled voice rasped. "And it is indeed Schmidt." The thief waved his pistol to indicate they were to move against the wall. "Don't try for that pistol, Reston."

Reston, the boys, and the two old men stood against the wall.

"You, the small boy, take that rope in the corner and tie up Reston. Quick!"

"Do it, Bob," Reston said.

Swallowing hard, Bob got the rope and tied Reston's hands and feet. Schmidt motioned him away and inspected Reston's bonds. Satisfied, the bandit stepped back.

"Now you boys tie the old men," the bandit ordered.

Jupiter and Bob tied Old Ben and Waldo. Then Bob tied Jupiter, and Schmidt himself tied up Bob. When they were all trussed up on the floor, the bandit stepped to the table and picked up the leather bag. His voice rasped mockingly.

"I must thank you for having the diamonds ready for me. You saved me all the trouble of digging them out after the earthquake. I've been watching them quite carefully, of course. I did not go to the trouble of stealing them to lose them that easily." The bandit chuckled. "You boys were a bit stubborn and troublesome, but when I saw those scuba tanks

I guessed what you were up to. I was a trifle nervous when I realized Reston was close behind me again, but it has all turned out fine."

The jewel thief bowed mockingly to his trussed victims, and vanished from the cabin.

Jupiter groaned. "I should have guessed he would be watching us! When he captured us in the cave it was obvious he knew about the digging— we could hear it from where he caught us."

"Don't blame yourself, Jupiter," Reston said. "You solved the entire case correctly. I should have realized myself that Schmidt was only using Old Ben and Waldo."

"Well," Bob said, "at least Jupe guessed right. The thief did return."

Jupiter frowned, unsatisfied. "What good is solving a mystery if you can't even see the villain's face?" he asked. "He'll get away, and we'll never know what he looks like. And Mr. Reston will have to start all over——"

Jupiter stopped in mid-sentence, his mouth open like a startled fish. He sat staring ahead as if in some kind of trance.

"Jupe?" Bob said.

"Jupiter," Sam Reston said, "what is it?"

Jupiter blinked as if he had just come back into the room from a long trip. "We've got to get loose!" he cried, straining at his bonds. "We've got to hurry and go after him!"

Sam Reston shook his head gloomily. "He's

long gone by now, Jupiter. He wouldn't stay around."

"I don't know," Jupiter said.

"You don't know what, Jupe?" asked Bob.

The sudden sound of horses' hoofs outside the cabin prevented Jupiter's reply. A moment later the outside door burst open, and a big man they had never seen before glared down at the five bound prisoners.

"What the devil is going on in here?" he boomed. "You boys should know better."

Bob and Jupe looked up at the big man, and then grinned with relief.

Behind him they saw the familiar and friendly faces of Pete and Mrs. Dalton.

18.
El Diablo Unmasked

The big man proved to be the sheriff of Santa Carla County, and at first he was very angry with the boys for trying to solve the mystery alone.

"Three boys have no business chasing a dangerous jewel thief!" the sheriff thundered.

"Anything might have happened in that cave," added Mrs. Dalton, "with all kinds of thieves and crazy men walking around! If Pete hadn't spotted those question marks and realized you might have gone to Old Ben's cabin, goodness knows how we would have found you!"

Bob looked a little bit sheepish, but Jupiter turned quickly to the sheriff.

"We're sorry, sir," he said politely, "but we did nothing really dangerous in the cave. We were most unfortunately captured by the thief Mr. Reston is pursuing."

Reston broke in. "That's right, sheriff. The boys had no way of knowing that there was a dangerous criminal in the cave. They thought they were merely solving the mystery of the moaning, and perhaps of a couple of eccentric but harmless old men. They had no idea of capturing a jewel thief until I came along. It was *my* idea to go after Old Ben and Waldo."

"And that's something I want to talk to you about later," the sheriff growled at Reston. "But maybe you're right. I guess the boys acted pretty responsibly all in all."

"I'd say more responsibly than most adults," Reston said, "And they seem to have solved our mystery, even if the thief did get away."

Mrs. Dalton smiled. "I'd say they have turned out to be pretty good investigators."

"They did solve the case at that," the sheriff went on. "It's too bad the thief got away, but we'll nab him yet."

"Please, sir!" Jupiter cried.

Everyone stared at the First Investigator in surprise.

"I'm not sure the thief *has* gotten away yet," Jupiter insisted eagerly, "or that he's even trying to."

"What do you mean, son?" asked the sheriff.

"Can you tell me where everyone else is, sir?" Jupiter asked quietly.

"Everyone else? You mean the people from the ranch? Why they're all out looking for you boys," the sheriff said. "Dalton and his men are down on the beach, and Luke Hardin and Professor Walsh are with some other men on the far side of Devil Mountain."

"Where were you going to meet later?" Jupiter asked.

"At the ranch house," replied the sheriff.

"Then I suggest we all go to the ranch house quickly," Jupiter said firmly.

The sheriff frowned. "Now see here, boy, if you have anything on your mind you better tell us."

Jupiter shook his head. "There isn't time, sir. It would take too long to explain, and we must catch him before he can dispose of the evidence."

"Better listen to the boy, Sheriff," Sam Reston advised. "I've learned from experience that he knows what he's talking about."

"All right then," the sheriff agreed. "Come on, boys, you can ride with us."

Jupiter got up behind the sheriff on his horse, and Bob and Pete rode with two deputies who had been waiting outside on horseback. It was a wild ride through the rugged ranchland. The boys hung on desperately, as they jounced and swayed along, unable to see where they were going.

But when they reached the house they saw no sign of life. There was only a dim light in the kitchen window.

"Well, son," the sheriff said to Jupiter, who clung behind him, "who did you expect to find here?"

Jupiter bit his lip in the dark. "I'm sure he will come back. We must have beaten him here. He has to pretend to search for us for a while, at least. I suggest we all dismount and wait in the dark."

"We'll dismount all right," the sheriff agreed, "but I want to know what this is all about."

The sheriff swung down, and helped Jupiter to the ground. A moment later Sam Reston pulled up in his car.

"Now, son," the sheriff said firmly, "you tell me what this wild goose chase is about."

"Well, sir," Jupiter explained, "I remembered some things the bandit said to us when we were in the cabin. I put them together with some facts, and . . ."

A man suddenly came limping toward them from the side of the ranch house.

"Well, I see you located them, Sheriff," Professor Walsh said. "Good work. You boys had quite a busy night, eh?"

The professor smiled from behind his thick glasses, and touched his left leg. "Took a spill, I'm afraid. Had to come back and bandage up a nasty cut on my leg."

"You're just in time, Professor," the sheriff said. "Young Jones here is about to tell us a story."

Jupiter's voice was calm. "That won't be necessary now, Sheriff. I suggest you search Professor

Walsh for the diamonds. I don't believe he would have abandoned them again, especially since he is sure we don't suspect that he is really Laslo Schmidt."

"Schmidt!" Sam Reston cried, staring at the professor.

"I think the diamonds will be under the bandage," Jupiter added.

With a cry, Professor Walsh turned and ran. In a second everyone was in pursuit. All except the boys and Mrs. Dalton. They turned and stared at Jupiter.

The First Investigator just stood there and grinned.

Hector Sebastian Hears a Story

"Jupe, were the diamonds really found under the bandage on Professor Walsh's leg?" Hector Sebastian asked.

"Yes, sir," Jupiter said. "They captured the professor just as he reached his car, the one with the Nevada license. It turned out that he had two cars. The one with the Nevada license he kept hidden in a concealed gully in Moaning Valley. The El Diablo costume and rubber mask were in that car. He had not disposed of them because he was confident that no one had guessed he was Laslo Schmidt."

"So his overconfidence did him in," the mystery writer observed. "Good work, guys."

It was a week after the capture of Professor

Walsh, alias Laslo Schmidt. The boys had just returned home after a well-earned week's vacation on
The Crooked-Y Ranch, where they swam, rode,
and learned about ranch operations. Now they
were sitting in the huge living room of Mr. Sebastian's house and were reporting on The Mystery of
the Moaning Cave from Bob's notes.

"Now I know why the cave moaned," Mr. Sebastian went on, "and what old Ben and Waldo
were up to. By the way, what happened to those two
old characters?"

Bob grinned. "The sheriff finally decided that
they really hadn't had a chance to be guilty of any
crime. He decided to believe they would eventually
have had the good sense to turn in the diamonds.
Mr. and Mrs. Dalton even forgave them for scaring
everyone."

Mr. Sebastian nodded, then puffed on his pipe
a moment. "I guess they were just carried away by
their dreams of a rich strike.

"And another thing," the novelist continued.
"I'm still foggy about how you suddenly realized
that El Diablo and Professor Walsh were really
Laslo Schmidt."

Jupiter leaned forward in his chair. "Well, I
began to wonder about Professor Walsh possibly
being the false El Diablo. Then it became clear that
Professor Walsh was the most logical person to be
Laslo Schmidt. He was the only real stranger at The

Crooked-Y, and his past was the most easily falsified."

Mr. Sebastian nodded. "I see that. He had been in the area for just a year and it's easier to pretend to be a professor than an ex-rodeo rider or a ranch foreman. But what made you suspect him at all?"

Jupiter frowned. "Actually, I should have suspected him sooner. But I admit it did not strike me until we all were captured in Old Ben's cabin. It was what he said after he tied us up that revealed it all to me."

"What he said?" Mr. Sebastian repeated with a raised eyebrow. He leafed through Bob's notes. "I don't remember him saying much."

"Not much, but enough," Jupiter answered. "First, he mentioned having seen our scuba tanks. Only someone at the ranch could have seen those tanks. Second, there was his voice. Although it was muffled and disguised so that we could not recognize it by its sound, he could not disguise his pattern of speech. And when I thought about my other clues, I suddenly realized the pattern was obviously that of Professor Walsh."

Mr. Sebastian's eyes sparkled. "Right. A person's speech pattern can be a real giveaway."

"Then," Jupiter went on, "he said that he had become nervous when he realized that Reston was close behind him again. That gave me two clues. One, that the false El Diablo knew who Mr. Reston was, and two, that he knew Mr. Reston was getting close to him!"

"Of course!" Mr. Sebastian exclaimed. "Reston had told you that Laslo Schmidt knew him by sight. And no one else had seen Reston except you guys. You *described* Reston to the others. But it was clear that the false El Diablo could recognize Reston, even with the eye patch and the scar."

"Exactly," Jupiter agreed.

"One problem, Jupe," the mystery novelist added. "All that is circumstantial. Those attributes fit Professor Walsh but they could also fit other people at the ranch. What made you zero in on Walsh?"

"The pistol he carried," Jupiter said triumphantly.

"What do you mean?" the writer asked, referring back to Bob's notes. "I didn't see anything here about the pistol—nothing special, I mean."

"No," Jupiter said quickly. "There was nothing special about the pistol itself, but about the way Walsh held it. You see, the El Diablo who captured us held the pistol in his left hand. He wore the holster on his left hip. But all the books and pictures indicated that El Diablo was right-handed. When we found the skeleton of the real El Diablo in the cave, it had the pistol in its right hand, too. So—"

"Good grief!" Mr. Sebastian interrupted, smacking himself on the forehead. "How could I have missed that! Of course. The professor was the only one with the theory that El Diablo was left-handed! He was tripped up by his own pet theory."

"Yes, sir, he was," Jupiter replied with a grin. "You see, he really *was* a professor as well as a thief. As Mr. Reston said, he had spent five years establishing another identity. He really was Professor Walsh, and he really was an expert on California history. He was actually writing a book about El Diablo, and when he impersonated the bandit he automatically conformed to his own theory and acted left-handed!"

Mr. Sebastian laughed uproariously. "Unbelievable. You boys really did a super job on this one. This may be your most cleverly deduced case yet. I'll be delighted to introduce it for you."

The boys all beamed happily at this high praise. Then Jupiter held out the old pistol that he and Pete had found in the hands of the real El Diablo.

"We thought you might like to have this as a memento of The Mystery of the Moaning Cave," Jupiter said.

"Will you look at that," Mr. Sebastian said with awe. "The pistol of the real El Diablo. I'll treasure this. Actually, you guys did a lot more than explain the moaning cave and solve the diamond robbery. You discovered the real ending of the legend of El Diablo."

"Wow!" Pete exclaimed. "We did, didn't we?"

"There's just one more loose end," Mr. Sebastian said, and his eyes twinkled. "Is there really an

Old One in that pool in the cave? Could *it* have killed El Diablo?"

Jupiter became thoughtful again. He stared out at the Pacific Ocean through Mr. Sebastian's huge picture windows.

"Well," Jupiter mused, "the legend of The Old One has been passed down for a long time. Possibly there is a true basis for it. It might be interesting to return to the cave and see if there is anything in that pool."

"Oh, no!" Bob and Pete groaned together.

But all Jupiter said then was, "Hmmmmm . . . I wonder."

The three boys filed out of the office, and Hector Sebastian looked at the pistol on his table and smiled. Once again The Three Investigators had explained a mystery that had baffled adults. He wondered what riddle they would tackle next. If Jupiter had his way, it might be The Old One in the cave. Bob and Pete might be smart to have their flashlights ready.

But whatever The Three Investigators probed next, it would definitely be a case of danger and suspense.

THE THREE INVESTIGATORS MYSTERY SERIES

NOVELS

The Secret of Terror Castle
The Mystery of the Stuttering Parrot
The Mystery of the Whispering Mummy
The Mystery of the Green Ghost
The Mystery of the Vanishing Treasure
The Secret of Skeleton Island
The Mystery of the Fiery Eye
The Mystery of the Silver Spider
The Mystery of the Screaming Clock
The Mystery of the Moaning Cave
The Mystery of the Talking Skull
The Mystery of the Laughing Shadow
The Secret of the Crooked Cat
The Mystery of the Coughing Dragon
The Mystery of the Flaming Footprints
The Mystery of the Nervous Lion
The Mystery of the Singing Serpent
The Mystery of the Shrinking House
The Secret of Phantom Lake
The Mystery of Monster Mountain
The Secret of the Haunted Mirror
The Mystery of the Dead Man's Riddle
The Mystery of the Invisible Dog
The Mystery of Death Trap Mine
The Mystery of the Dancing Devil
The Mystery of the Headless Horse
The Mystery of the Magic Circle
The Mystery of the Deadly Double
The Mystery of the Sinister Scarecrow
The Secret of Shark Reef
The Mystery of the Scar-Faced Beggar
The Mystery of the Blazing Cliffs
(*Continued on next page*)

The Mystery of the Purple Pirate
The Mystery of the Wandering Cave Man
The Mystery of the Kidnapped Whale
The Mystery of the Missing Mermaid
The Mystery of the Two-Toed Pigeon
The Mystery of the Smashing Glass
The Mystery of the Trail of Terror
The Mystery of the Rogues' Reunion
The Mystery of the Creep-Show Crooks

FIND YOUR FATE™ MYSTERIES

The Case of the Weeping Coffin
The Case of the Dancing Dinosaur

PUZZLE BOOKS

The Three Investigators' Book of Mystery Puzzles